The *weight* of a *woman*

Printed in Australia

First Printing: June 2022

Shawline Publishing Group Pty Ltd
www.shawlinepublishing.com.au

Paperback ISBN- 9781922751331

Ebook ISBN- 9781922751386

 A catalogue record for this
book is available from the
National Library of Australia

The
weight
of a
woman

tansy
BOGGON

ALSO BY TANSY BOGGON

NON-FICTION

*Joyful Eating: How to Break Free of Diets and
Make Peace with Your Body*

CHILDREN'S BOOKS

The Superheroes on Your Plate

Your weight and body do not define you

Author's Note

The Weight of a Woman is a lighter version of my self-help book, Joyful Eating: How to Break Free of Diets and Make Peace with Your Body. It is an entirely fictional story, written to be an entertaining bedtime or beachside read. But it is also the story of many women, maybe even yourself.

If you're looking to embark on a journey similar to Jenni's, but you don't have a character like Norelle to guide you, you may find Joyful Eating helpful. However, if you find anything in this book emotionally triggering, I encourage you to seek guidance and support from a suitably qualified counsellor or therapist who can assist you with weight or eating concerns.

Prologue

Jenni feels the breeze sweeping through her hair and the soft sand under her feet and between her toes. She takes a moment to enjoy these sensations. Then, she deeply inhales the salty air and slips off her sheer kaftan. She instantly feels her skin tingle as the fresh air envelops her body. She feels so alive. Alive in a way that she hasn't for a long time.

She gently submerges her body in the water, immersing herself in the sensory experience of the moment. She feels calm and at peace. She feels a sense of liberation.

She momentarily remembers a time when she would not have ventured into the water. A time when she would not dare take off her kaftan for fear of exposing her body. She recollects all the times she would sit on the beach and watch others frolic and play while feeling jealous and resentful of others' *perfect* bodies and freedom. Yet now, she's let that go.

She lifts her feet off the sand and allows the water to take her weight. She stretches out her legs and floats on the surface, fully supported by the ocean. Her body is buoyant.

She ponders how many things she has postponed until she had the body she desired, until her body was *good enough*.

Jenni draws her attention back to the sensory experience of the moment. She feels her hair floating around her head and the lapping water gently caressing her body. As tears begin to well up, she feels the warmth beneath her eyelids. She traces her tears as they roll down the sides of her face to merge with the ocean.

Yet, they are not tears of sadness. They are tears of joy. Joy for the sense of freedom she feels in her body without shame. Joy to feel the aliveness within her again.

Chapter 1

"The story you tell yourself—forms the lens through which you see your body and relate with food."

—Joyful Eating

∽

Jenni stretches out her arm to turn off the alarm clock and then reaches for her phone to begin her morning ritual of scrolling through her Facebook feed in bed. It is a morning routine that has become second nature, and the feeling it evokes in her the same day-in-day-out.

She scrolls. A pregnancy announcement. Wedding pictures from a high school classmate. A promotion at work. An exotic holiday. A flawless meal. Motivational quotes.

Jenni wants to *catch up* with the world, yet each morning she feels deflated by the time her feet touch the floor; she does not have a partner, a baby, a promotion, a planned holiday, photogenic meals—and most notably, she doesn't have a photogenic body. She doesn't have a body that she is prepared to display on Facebook: a body that is ready for any of these things.

Each morning she makes her way to the bathroom, where she looks at herself in the mirror after washing her hands.

She then dampens her face and inspects the puffiness of her cheeks.

Her morning alarm not only signals a call for her to wake, it signals yet another day of constant contemplation of what to eat. The daily grind begins with breakfast.

Jenni decides to skip breakfast, as she has to get to work early. She's *volunteered* to set up for the longer than usual quarterly staff meeting postponed to the day back after the October long weekend.

Thus, it's no surprise she is the first to the office, a two-storey building with the lower level used as the public space. It is where the downstairs staff support clientele with enquires about the credit union's services.

There is an information desk at the entrance, a row of service desks at the far back wall and three small glass offices along one side where the loans and insurance staff meet with clientele. The office space is light and airy. Citrus colours accentuate the mostly black and white space. *Oh, how the times have changed*, Jenni thinks as she steps into the open space. It is a long way removed from the days of dark carpet and heavy wood.

However, Jenni doesn't work here. No, she is not downstairs staff. She works upstairs in the management office, tucked away and hidden from the clientele. Although there is a glass wall along one side where, should clientele look up, they can see sleek meeting rooms. Jenni's workspace is tucked behind a wall that extends out above the service desks.

She mostly shares the hidden workspace with Pam, her full-time work companion and ally in the office. It is a space where all the unsightly stuff is kept—paper supplies, photocopier, filing cabinets and other miscellaneous items—including her and Pam. Except for Wednesdays, when the efficient and evasive Amanda comes in to support Pam with payroll.

Amanda, who doesn't come in on Tuesdays, had asked Jenni to set up and place flyers about personality types on the chairs for the quarterly staff meeting. Amanda is not easy to say no to, and thus Jenni is there early setting up.

೦౦

In her own world, Jenni hums to herself while she positions chairs when Barry, the Loans Manager, walks in. She checks the clock behind the information desk. It's 20 minutes till the meeting starts. 'You're early,' she states.

'Couldn't wait to start after the long weekend,' he replies sarcastically.

'Me neither. I even *volunteered* to set up for Amanda,' she smirks, air-quoting the word volunteer.

'Oh, I understand.' He raises his eyebrows in agreement. 'Can I help you?'

'I think I've got everything under control.' She smiles at Barry, noticing how clean-shaven and fresh he looks this morning.

Barry is considered a floater staff. He meets with clientele in the glass offices downstairs, and when he's not with clients, he works on his laptop in one of the upstairs glass meeting rooms. *He must be deemed good looking enough to be seen behind the company's window lettering*, Jenni thinks, glancing toward him as he inspects the display of instant coffee, tea bags and packaged biscuits. He runs his index finger along the table as if itemising everything on it.

'I think I'm going to need real coffee this morning,' he announces. 'Would you like one?'

'No, thanks. I'd better keep with it.' Jenni continues shuffling chairs.

'You sure? It's no trouble.'

'I'm sure.' She shoots him a smile. 'Thanks, Barry.'

He leaves her alone in the office.

⌀

She isn't alone long. Ten minutes after Barry leaves, a few staff begin to arrive.

Jenni finds herself talking to Becca while the others mill about the drink and snack table. Becca is the office's unofficial health and fitness guru. She's always up with the latest superfood and fitness craze.

Becca had walked in, seen the snacks on the table and declared things would have to change with the offerings at staff meetings. She is now going to be one hundred per cent sugar-free. Jenni mistakenly asks what that means precisely—would she still be eating honey and fruits, or is that out of bounds too?

'Sugar is the cause of so many health issues, like depression, migraines, autoimmune diseases and even cancer,' Becca explains, 'it's evil, in that the more we eat it, the more we want it. The only way to liberate ourselves of its addictive properties is to quit it entirely. So that's my plan for this month, and ongoing most probably. Why would I want to go back to eating poison ever again?' Becca holds Jenni's gaze in a knowing way, as if what she's said is plainly obvious.

Why, indeed? Jenni thinks. *Because it tastes good? Because I have no control over my eating? Because I don't want to give up one of life's pleasures?*

Becca clearly doesn't notice Jenni's mind is elsewhere. 'You should join me, Jenni. It would be so good for you, and I can help keep you accountable.'

Why do people feel they can give me unsolicited advice? Jenni fumes to herself, feeling her body tense. It is, however, apparent. People clearly think she needs to and thus, would want to lose weight.

'Um… I'm not sure I want to give up sugar entirely.' Jenni says while thinking; *I'm not sure I ever could.*

Nevertheless, Becca is convincing. Not just because of what she says, but the conviction with which she says it. And mostly, it is because Becca is slender, bouncy, confident and uninhibited. She is everything Jenni is not.

⟳

Jenni looks around the room to see if she can *save herself* from Becca. She notices Barry has returned. He is holding a takeaway coffee cup and a small brown paper bag. When he catches her looking his way, he grins and raises his cup as if to say cheers. She smiles. *He is such a goofy guy*, she thinks.

Then behind him, Priya, the Branch Manager, walks through the front door. She moves in a determined way as she always does, as if on a mission, which the beginning of a financial quarter would only amplify. Jenni knows she'll want to *excite* them for the quarter ahead.

The meeting goes exactly as Jenni anticipates. It is mostly projections and key performance indicators, splashed with some motivational talk to *pump them up.*

The only thing that surprises Jenni is the plans to give back to the community. The credit union is going to employ a Community Outreach Officer to manage sponsorship of activities in collaboration with local libraries, schools and sporting groups. It sounds very charitable, but the intention is more likely to increase visibility and thus clientele.

When the meeting ends, and the doors are opened to the public, Jenni makes her way up the stairs to her office behind the wall. Despite the assertiveness of the meeting, as the Accounts Payable Officer, little will change in her role.

Jenni begins shuffling through her in-tray as her computer

loads up. She is so focused on sorting papers she doesn't notice that Barry has followed her. He is still holding the small brown paper bag. 'I know you didn't want anything, but I got you a little something when I bought my coffee,' he pauses, 'however, when I got back...' He nods in the direction of the service desks downstairs where Becca is stationed. 'It was kinda... you know.'

Jenni smiles as he hands her the bag. She cautiously pries it open. Inside is a single melting moment biscuit.

'They looked so delicious. I bought two. I ate mine in the mind-numbing meeting,' he confesses.

Jenni is gobsmacked. 'Thanks, Barry,' she says, forcing a smile. *What was he thinking? So, he bought the fat girl a biscuit. After all, that's what fat girls eat, right?* She doesn't know what to think. She holds the bag like it is a bag people take walking to pick up after their dogs.

Barry is clearly confused by her expression and body language. 'It's absolutely delicious,' he declares, 'you'll love it.' He affectionately taps her desk before moving away.

'I'm sure it is,' Jenni agrees, placing it beside her computer. 'Thanks, Barry. I'll have it later.'

She has absolutely no intention of eating it. It probably contains more calories than a small meal, and it most definitely violates Becca's sugar-free health kick. Jenni knows she has to gain control over her diet, and she doesn't need others making it any tougher for her.

She tries her hardest all morning to ignore that melting moment. She imagines its softness, its buttery flavour, its sweetness and crumbly texture. It is obvious to her she has to stop eating food like this if she has any chance of losing the weight she so desperately wants.

However, as the hours pass, it feels like that melting moment is *calling out* to her, continually pulling her attention to it. In frustration, she takes the bag and places it in her top drawer, out of sight. She's going to eat healthy today. *I'll eat a salad for lunch and no afternoon snack, she tells herself.*

She has to incite immense willpower not to dip her hand into the drawer and gobble up the biscuit. And she manages it! She gets through her workday without eating the biscuit. She doesn't succumb to temptation.

She can't, however, let the melting moment go to waste. So, as she packs for the day, she places the brown paper bag into her handbag.

Then, while waiting for her train, she feels an immense wave of hunger. She won't be home for another hour, and then she has to make dinner. She reaches her hand into her handbag and feels for the paper bag. She deserves a treat to reward herself for not giving in to temptation all day.

She looks up and down the platform to see if anyone is watching. Then she snatches the biscuit and stuffs half of it into her mouth. Oh, it is so delicious. She so deserves this.

Jenni chews quickly, looking around her but not wanting to make eye contact with anyone. She hates people seeing her eat. She knows people assume that is all she does.

Then, with a sense of relief, she swallows. Then pushes the other half into her mouth.

She is relieved the biscuit is finally gone—it can no longer occupy her thoughts. And she is relieved to have put something in her growling stomach. Yet, she is still hungry. The tiny salad at lunchtime had barely filled her, and now, four hours later, she is ravenous. This is a common occurrence for Jenni; to withhold food and eat *healthy* all day only to come home so hungry she wants to eat anything she can get her hands on. She has to stop this. *I have to gain control over my eating*; she admits to herself.

～

On her walk from the train station home, Jenni notices a banner fluttering outside a gym she passes every day. In bold lettering, it says, "Summer-Beach Body Challenge". It is literally a *sign*. So, she decides to go in.

As she enters, Jenni is overwhelmed by the loud music and whirring of exercise machines. She notices the wall to ceiling mirrors along one side of the gym where people are peddling bikes, looking at themselves. *Maybe that's what you do when you look gorgeous—you can't stop checking yourself out*, she thinks.

She heads to reception, where a young woman wearing tight leggings and a top bunched up at her waist to show off her flat stomach is standing. *Oh, here we go*, Jenni thinks. *Not my sort of place, but maybe, just maybe, I'll find what I'm looking for. It's worth a shot.*

'Welcome to Inspired Life Gym. How can I help you?' the young lady chirps with a touch too much enthusiasm.

'Um, I'm wondering about the Summer-Beach Body Challenge you have advertised out the front,' Jenni stammers.

'Are you looking to lose weight?' the receptionist asks, handing Jenni a pamphlet.

Duh, is she blind? Jenni feels like saying, but goes with, 'Most definitely. I've decided that enough is enough.'

'Good on you!' the receptionist exclaims. 'The Summer-Beach Body Challenge will definitely help you shed excess weight, and we also have some awesome personal training programs that we can run through with you.'

Jenni interjects, 'No, I'm not interested in an exercise program right now. Just diet support.'

'Oh, but if you really want to lose weight, it is essential that you exercise, too. It is a requirement for you to enter the Summer-Beach Body Challenge that you meet with one of our personal trainers for an assessment.' Before Jenni can object, she calls out behind her, 'Justin, this lady is interested in the Summer-Beach Body Challenge.'

Jenni wants to dive for cover as an athletic-looking man comes out through a door behind the counter. 'Oh, I didn't mean today... I... I just wanted to know more about the challenge.' Jenni looks to the young lady for reprieve.

'We can just have a chat today,' Justin says, 'we can talk about your goals, take some measurements and do a fitness assessment to determine where to start.'

A fitness assessment. Measurements. Fuck! Abort mission! Jenni has to get out of here. 'I'm sorry, not today,' she winces.

'No worries. We can schedule a time if you like,' Justin continues.

'Ah no, that's okay.' Jenni takes a step back. 'I'll think about it and come back another time.'

Jenni dashes out of the gym and power walks towards her apartment. What was she thinking—going into a place like that? A place where they want to measure and assess her, give her goals to strive for and exercise and meal plans that would undoubtedly take over her life. She can't go down that road again. She absolutely can't.

Jenni has been here before—innumerable times. She's had the promises. She's gone all out to achieve her goals, only to end up heavier than when she started. What is wrong with her? How can little miss tight pants and Justin have these trim bodies? How can they have figured it out, and she hasn't?

On arriving home, her mood deflated, Jenni microwaves a frozen pizza and plops down in front of the TV. Before she knows it, the entire family size pizza is gone. Not because she particularly enjoyed its limp, rubbery texture. It is there is nothing else to do, and she can't be bothered making anything better.

Deflated and defeated, having devoured the entire pizza, Jenni makes her way back to the kitchen to throw out the pizza box. The last thing she wants is to wake up to the smell of failure.

She runs her plate under the tap and then goes to take the pizza box, along with her other recycling, down to the recycle bin. She carries the recycling crate perched on her jiggling belly. She then notices the pamphlet from the gym. Her gaze falls to the words: "is your weight holding you back?" *Sure is,* Jenni thinks as the contents clatter into the apartment's recycle bin.

For the rest of the week, Jenni busies herself with her regular routine: wake, work, eat, eat too much, fall asleep in front of the TV and drag herself to bed to do it all again. She tries to ignore the nagging thought her life could and should be more than this. That would mean getting her weight under control—a daunting task she's been unsuccessfully trying to achieve since she left Paul five years ago.

Jenni and Paul met at university. They were both studying in the Faculty of Economics and Finances and had overlaps in subjects. At first, they were simply studying partners for some subjects. They then began to eat their lunches together on campus and, with time, would get together in the evenings and weekends for meals or to watch movies. Their relationship developed incrementally, founded more so on it making sense than being passionate or impulsive.

Paul had loved Jenni deeply. However, he never made her feel like she was special. At the time, however, she simply felt lucky to have found someone who loved her.

Although they were both studying finances, Jenni was never as clear or determined on the career path she wanted to take as Paul had been. While he'd become a fully-fledged accountant at a firm, Jenni worked a few finance support roles on leaving university. She didn't enjoy the pressure of business and having to find clients or be responsible for other people's money. She loved being helpful and putting things in order. She definitely wasn't a risk-taker.

Not that Paul was much of a risk-taker, either. He was just more certain of the career trajectory he was on. His certainty stemmed from his preoccupation with doing what he thought he should do—living up to others' expectations of him. Consequently, he became incredibly busy in his work to exceed targets and climb the corporate ladder.

After leaving university and both starting full-time work, they had little time together, and when they did, it was mostly watching TV. Their lives became a predictable routine of work, TV, sleep.

On the weekends, Paul often said he was too exhausted to go out to the park together or do other activities, which Jenni would wrack her brain to think up. She had begun to wonder whether it was they had little in common—little to talk about or do together. However, if she suggested this to him, he'd tell her he was content with the way things were—that they were working towards their future and financial freedom.

Jenni feared he was just settling. She knew Paul loved her, but she felt there must be more to life.

And then there was the elephant in the room he never wanted to talk about—her weight. If she asked him about it, he'd roll his eyes as if to say, *not this again.* He said her weight was not an issue for him, and he loved her the way she was. However, she wondered if their relationship could have been different—more exciting—if she were slim.

Paul was supportive of her weight loss efforts, but he never encouraged her. It was as if he knew she'd fail.

His disinterest in her weight loss attempts made her so angry. Countless times she'd say to him, 'You're dismissive of this diet because you don't think I can do it.' And his response would be some variation of, 'It's not that, Jen. It's just... I don't think you need to. You're beautiful as you are. And I hate seeing you putting yourself through all these restrictive programs.'

Although sympathetic words, they were not reassuring, mostly because she didn't believe them. 'You're only saying that because you've got me now. It's easier to stay with me than find someone else,' she'd retort.

'No, I'm with you because I love who you are,' he'd dispute.

Then she'd snap at him, 'But not how I look. You just put up with that.'

At this point in these all-to-common conversations, frustration would begin to show on his face. 'Not at all, Jen. I think you're beautiful,' he'd say.

Yet her frustration would cause her to believe and respond, 'But you could love me more.'

'I'm not sure that could be possible, hun.' Yet his reassurance never came with the gentleness that would lead Jenni to truly believe it. Instead, it would do more to reinforce her resolve to lose weight. *We'll see about that,* she'd think, wanting to prove him wrong.

She started to believe his resignation to just settling was squashing her ability to live her life to the fullest. She felt he was holding her back. He believed their relationship was solid and was prepared to take the next logical steps—marriage and children. He reasoned that making this commitment and beginning a family would give them both a greater sense of purpose. And he assured her nothing needed to change for that to happen.

Although Jenni wanted more from life than to settle down with Paul, she stayed with him for years, even once the flame had dimmed, mostly because she was unsure anyone else would love her as he did. Her parents' comments reinforced the idea she was 'lucky to have Paul' and 'Paul is such a lovely man.' It was true, Paul was a lovely man, but she wanted more from life. She wanted to feel excited about life. She wanted adventure and to experience life fully. She wasn't sure how or what exactly, yet she came to believe staying with Paul was stifling her.

After nearly thirteen years together, as she approached her thirty-fifth birthday, Jenni finally decided to leave Paul to *find herself*. And she knew exactly where to start—by losing the kilos that had only increased during her relationship with him. She thought if she felt lighter, she would be freer to do what she wanted in life. Step one—shed the weight.

And now, with her fortieth birthday looming less than six months away, Jenni feels this is her last chance to lose the weight once and for all. She knows she probably wouldn't be able to lose all the weight she wants by her birthday. But if she could see her weight dropping week-by-week, she feels she'd be somewhat hopeful of achieving the goal she had set out to reach five years prior.

That night, Jenni devises a meal plan that involves a diet shake for lunch and cutting out carbs at dinner. She knows how much she struggles to follow a diet. So, the plan she puts together is something she feels she could continue for the next six months— until she starts seeing some promising results.

Chapter 2

"No amount of resisting what is, blame or guilt will change your body in this moment."

—Joyful Eating

The following week, towards the end of another draining day in the office, Jenni loses concentration when she hears the singsong of a cooee coming up the stairs. *Who could that be?* she thinks.

Jenni glances up to see a slim woman in her mid-fifties with cropped white hair. The woman isn't wearing the customer service uniform or smart casual attire of the upstairs staff. No, this woman oozes eccentricity.

She wears jeans and a purple cap-sleeved top, with an overlay teal apron dress speckled with paint splatters. Jenni's jaw drops. *Who is this quirky artist type, and what is she doing up here?* Jenni scours the office for someone to explain.

'Hiya, you must be Jenni.' The lady stretches out her spindly paint speckled hand. Seeing Jenni's confusion, she continues, 'I'm Norelle, the Community Outreach Officer.'

Oh, that explains a lot, Jenni thinks. 'Lovely to meet you, Norelle.'

'You too. I'm in a bit of a rush.' Norelle gives an apologetic smile. 'I need to raise a purchase order for some paint,' she explains, 'I'm working with a school that is painting a mural alongside the M3. I need to get them some more paint before they start back tomorrow.'

'Oh, okay,' Jenni says, taking the paperwork from Norelle. Then she asks, 'You've got this signed off by Priya?'

'Yep, just here.' Norelle shuffles through the papers.

'Okay, I'll just be a few moments.' Jenni taps away at her computer.

'Thanks, you're a lifesaver,' Norelle says, relieved.

'No worries,' Jenni murmurs as she double-checks the paperwork and puts the payment through.

'So, how long have you worked here, Jenni?' Norelle chirps.

'Seven years in this office. Before that, I worked in the South Brisbane branch.'

'Wow, so you've been with the Union a while then,' Norelle states.

'Yep,' Jenni says, eyes still on her computer.

'So, you're a great person to come to for advice and inside information then,' Norelle comments.

'No, not really. I pretty much keep to myself, tucked away up here. I'm more of a behind-the-scenes person—keep the place ticking without being seen,' Jenni says matter-of-factly. However, the smile on her face is not one of contentment, but resignation. Although being hidden away is something Jenni has become accustomed to, she wants to be seen—to be worthy of being seen. However, her body prohibits her from that. It has for most of her life.

☙

For as long as she could remember, Jenni had been larger than other girls. However, in her early years of primary school, it hadn't been an issue. She'd play with the other kids—riding her bike, swimming in the creek just outside of town and playing school sports.

When she was ten, she became aware that her body size was an issue among her peers. And although she received cruel comments about her weight, more hurtful were her friends talking about their bodies in a denigrating way. If their bodies weren't good enough, what did that mean about her body?

Almost overnight, the girls began comparing their bodies and commenting on how other girls and women looked. Jenni felt like the odd one out. Not only because her body was different, but because she could never engage in the conversations.

In year seven, Jenni drifted away from her friends and found herself hanging out more with Jake. Jake lived two streets away. They'd played together when younger, along with the other kids, but as she drifted from her girlfriends, she and Jake became a duo.

In their first year of high school, they were inseparable. They hung out after school most days. They'd ride their bikes and swim together. They'd talk and listen to music.

Then they spent the entire summer holiday together. They'd lie under the stars, gazing into the night sky, sharing their fears and dreams, talking as if their lives were to be forever intertwined. He was her best friend.

Early in their second year of high school, Jenni started to think maybe Jake and she were more than just friends. Boys and girls had started *going out* and declaring one another girlfriend and boyfriend. Jenni daren't ask Jake if they were going out. But it wasn't long before the other kids assumed they were.

Then at school, Jake began spending more of his time with the guys. If Jenni walked past him when he was with them, they'd laugh and make comments like, 'Jake, isn't that your g-i-r-l friend' and 'Hey, Jake likes b-i-g girls.'

To Jenni's dismay, Jake didn't refute their comments or even acknowledge her. Although this hurt, Jenni understood the pressures of school. She just looked forward to each afternoon when they could hang out after classes were finished, without others' judgement and remarks. When they were alone, no one else in the world mattered—she could be herself with him.

As the months passed, Jenni would occasionally ask Jake why he didn't acknowledge their friendship with the boys at school or stand up for her. He'd shrug it off as unimportant and say it was just a *guy thing*. He'd tell her it was more straightforward if they kept their friendship an out-of-school thing.

Jenni couldn't imagine life without Jake. If being with him meant they had to ignore one another at school, she'd do it.

As the second year of high school continued, they kept their friendship secret. Jenni relished the school holidays when they could be together all the time without having to pretend. However, unlike when they were younger, most of their time was spent indoors, away from prying eyes.

Behind closed doors, they'd listen to music, read to one another, watch movies, lie on the carpet staring at the ceiling, sharing their fears and dreams. Then one evening, towards the end of the summer holidays, before they'd start their third year of high school, Jake tentatively placed his hand on hers. Then with time, when they'd be lying on the couch or carpet listening to music or watching a movie, his hand would stray under her shirt or between her legs. Jenni wouldn't move or say a word. She wanted Jake to want her. She desperately wanted to be more than his friend. However, before long, the new school year started, as did the same pattern of being ignored during the school day.

Jenni desperately wanted Jake to acknowledge they were more than friends. Everyone knew they hung out, but he denied there was anything more. Yet, at night after school, his hands and his body would tell another story.

Jenni accepted it was easier for Jake if they kept the intimacy between them secret. She was well aware the other boys and for that matter, the girls too, thought she wasn't someone anyone would want to go out with. However, she began resenting being his secret; his big fat secret.

As the school year's end approached, Jenni hoped she would be his date for the Year 10 prom. She was utterly devastated when she heard rumours at school that Jake was taking Nikki. Nikki was not a popular girl, but she was slim. She looked exactly how a girlfriend should.

Jenni was heartbroken and ashamed of herself. She hated herself as much as she hated Jake. And so, she pushed him away and started her first diet. She resolved to show him what he'd lost and maybe, just maybe, he would come back to her.

He never did.

And her weight never changed all that much, despite her best efforts. And so, she spent the remainder of high school, either on or off a diet, watching Jake going out with other girls— thin girls—while she was never good enough to be anyone's girlfriend.

Jenni is shaken from her thoughts. 'I know, I didn't expect to find anyone hidden away up here.' Norelle indicates the confined office space—if you could call it that.

'I'm used to it.' Jenni shrugs.

'You should join me on one of my community visits,' Norelle continues, 'each staff member is allowed four days a year out on community activities. We'll have to schedule a time for you to join me.'

Norelle clearly didn't get the memo that I should stay tucked away, Jenni reflects. 'Sure,' she responds half-heartily.

'Now, you'll need to get Priya to put that through,' she instructs, handing Norelle a copy of the paperwork.

'Thanks, Jenni. I'm struggling to get my head around all these internal processes. Let's catch up soon and you can select an activity to join me on,' Norelle sings as she dashes away. *Clearly, she has no problem being seen,* Jenni contemplates as she scrutinises Norelle's conspicuous outfit, which is so out of place here in this stifling office.

⌒

On her way from work to the train station, Jenni notices a familiar figure on the opposite side of the road. He waves. *Oh fuck,* she thinks, unable to now pretend she hasn't seen him. It is Paul... and he is... pushing a pram. *What the hell,* Jenni thinks, as she stands motionless, watching Paul cross at the crosswalk and make his way over to her.

'Hi, Jenni,' he says with the pram between them, preventing any need for an obligatory hug.

'Hi, Paul.' Jenni nods toward the baby. 'So... so you and Shelly...?' She is unable to release the remainder of the words she wants to say.

'Yes,' Paul beams, 'can you believe it? We've now had a baby and, and... we're engaged to be married this summer.' Paul can barely contain himself as Jenni attempts to find the words to express her... whatever the emotion is she's feeling.

She is dumbfounded. She shakes her head and puts on a brave face. 'Wow, Paul. That's... incredible... uh, fantastic. Congratulations. You look so happy... congratulations.'

'Thanks, Jenni. I'm happier than you could ever believe. I never knew how much I wanted to be a father. I'm over the moon in love with this little one,' he says, bending down to rub the baby's chubby cheeks.

'Great,' Jenni says half-heartedly as she attempts to shake the constriction in her chest.

He looks up at her. 'And you? How are you?'

'Oh, great, couldn't be better,' she says on autopilot.

Paul doesn't seem to notice her unenthusiastic response, as he is clearly enthralled with his little cherub. He then straightens up. 'I'm really pleased,' he says sincerely, looking her directly in the eye, 'I hope you've gotten everything you wanted?'

'Uh-huh,' she responds, 'I've really got to get going, or I'll miss my train.' She takes a step backward, away from him and the baby.

'No worries, Jenni. It was lovely to see you.' He bends forward as if to kiss her and then pulls back, giving her a gentle squeeze on the shoulder. 'All the best, Jen.'

'You... you too,' she says, turning and making her way into the tunnel entrance to the train station.

He's got a fucking baby, she thinks. *He's so fucking happy.* She struggles to hold back the tears as the thoughts whirl around her brain. She makes her way through the tunnel, head down, wondering where she'd gone wrong. She no longer has feelings for Paul, but their relationship hadn't been bad. He'd loved her. It was her... her that was broken—her and her fucking body. *Fuck, who am I kidding?* she thinks as she contemplates what chance she has of losing this weight.

'Watch it, lady,' a voice snaps at her as she's blocked a group of teenage boys coming down the stairs. She steps to the side, head down and doesn't say a word.

Oh, she's been watching it—her weight, that is—for as long as she can remember and this is where it had got her: single, fat and approaching forty. *What is the point of these diets?* she wonders. They don't work; they never had. She is so far from her goal weight. So far from the life she dreamed of living—the life she'd thought Paul and her weight had been holding her back from.

Jenni can't be bothered to do anything when she gets home; even heating hot chips seems like too much effort. So, she pries open a bag of Cheezels and climbs straight into bed. *Is this it? Is this really my fucking life?* she thinks with despair.

She scrolls through her Facebook feed, poking Cheezel after Cheezel into her mouth. *What is the fucking point?* she thinks… and then, she comes upon a sponsored post that grabs her attention.

Although she can make an appointment online, Jenni feels that given the gravity of the decision she's about to make; she's more comfortable talking to a receptionist to schedule a time. At work the next day, she steps into one of the meeting rooms while Pam is in the bathroom to make the call.

'Good morning, Sunshine Weight Loss Solutions. You're speaking with Deb. How can I bring sunshine into your day?'

'Umm… Hi Deb. I want to make an appointment with a surgeon to discuss my options.'

'Oh, it's wonderful you're looking to take control of your weight. Do you have a referral from your GP?'

'Umm, no. Do I need one?'

'Oh, no. It's not necessary to have a referral,' Deb reassures. 'It's just sometimes doctors refer to us and give a bit of medical history that can help get the process started. Have you read through the criteria on our website?'

'Yep. I'm pretty sure I qualify,' Jenni confirms quickly.

'Great. We ask that you complete and submit an initial consultation form before your appointment, anyway. We have an opening with Dr Johnson next Tuesday at 11 am. Does that work for you?'

Jenni hesitates a moment; it all sounds so… medical… so… serious.

'Umm... I'll have to see if I can get the morning off work. Can I book it and then get back to you if I need to change it?'

'Sure. We do have a cancellation policy. So, if you could confirm sooner rather than later, that would be best for us both.'

'Okay. Book me in and I'll let you know if there is a problem,' Jenni says before Deb outlines the consultation and documentation she'll need to bring.

Jenni feels a sense of excitement and nervousness as she hangs up the phone: this is it—she's taking action to lose her excess weight. She heads straight downstairs to the client meeting room where Priya is working. She tentatively knocks on the door. 'Morning,' Jenni gives Priya a questioning smile.

'Come in. What is it, Jenni?' Priya looks at her with concern.

'Oh, there is no problem. I know I haven't submitted a time off request form. But, I've... I've tentatively made an appointment at a weight loss surgery place next Tuesday morning, and am... umm, wondering if I can take the morning off?' Jenni gives a forced smile.

'Are you having a procedure?' Priya asks.

'No. No, it's just the initial consultation to discuss my eligibility and options.' Jenni confirms.

'Good on you, Jenni!' Priya exclaims, surprising Jenni. 'It's great you're taking matters into your own hands. I had a staff member have weight loss surgery a few years back and they had wonderful results. They were like an entirely new person.'

Jenni nods.

'I just asked when,' Priya continues, 'as my understanding is if you go ahead with the surgery, you'll need at least two weeks off work.'

'Oh, okay. I don't really know much about it yet,' Jenni admits.

'No worries. Just let me know as soon as you know the surgery date,' Priya says in a somewhat commanding tone before confirming her reasoning, 'so that we can ensure we're covered for your time off.'

'Absolutely,' Jenni assures.

Priya continues, 'I believe you have some time in lieu owing. So, if you can get the paperwork to me by lunch today, we can put it through. I'm happy for you, Jenni. This is a positive step.'

'Thanks,' Jenni says, stepping out of the room, not wanting to take up any more of Priya's precious time.

That evening, Jenni downloads the intake form and begins entering her details for the weight loss clinic. The initial questions stimulate no emotional response. However, others do.

She feels no emotional charge entering her name, address, phone number or Medicare card. However, in entering her age, 39, her relationship status, single, number of dependents, zero, a feeling of dejection washes over her. She's nearly forty and still single, with no prospects of children anytime soon, maybe never.

Her height holds no emotion. It is simply a measure of how tall she is, 1.63 m. Her weight, now that is another matter entirely. Or at least it has been in the past.

Jenni decides she'd better enter her precise weight, so she makes her way to the bathroom. She hops on the bathroom scales as she has many times before, with either a feeling of dread or hopefulness. However, right now, the emotion she feels is more optimistic. For whatever her weight is, she is now going to change it.

She enters the figure into the form and sits back down at the kitchen table to complete the remaining questions; allergies, medications, medical history, family history. She attempts to read the fine print and then watches the videos on the Sunshine Weight Loss Solutions website, explaining the types of bariatric surgery they offer. She then makes herself a fresh salad for dinner, feeling that this is the fresh start she's been hungry for.

❦

On the morning of her consultation at the weight loss clinic, Jenni sleeps in and enjoys her breakfast on her apartment's small balcony. It is a rare occurrence for her to eat out there. However, this morning she feels like she is ready to begin living her life differently: a life where she is in the driver's seat, not her weight.

She is also not in a rush as she plans on taking an Uber. However, as she begins to enter the address into the Uber app, she realises she doesn't want the driver to know where she is going. So, she goes onto Google to select a legitimate business nearby and then enters the address for a pet shop. She feels more comfortable being seen as a cat lady than having a stranger's sympathy for being a fat lady heading to a weight loss clinic.

She soon regrets her choice when she finds herself making small talk with the chatty and inquisitive Uber driver about a pet she doesn't have and then has to walk the two blocks in the late morning heat. By the time she reaches the characterless three-storey glass building, she is sweaty and tense; she is about to make one of the biggest decisions of her life.

Jenni pulls open the heavy glass door and steps into the cool air conditioning. She immediately feels a physical sense of relief as the cool air envelops her body, although it doesn't alleviate her nervousness. She takes in the equally cold décor.

The reception and waiting area have the look of a display home with clean lines and gleaming white surfaces. It doesn't have an ounce of homeliness to make her feel comfortable in this somewhat clinical building. She continues toward the counter, feeling the stickiness of her armpits as she provides her name to the neatly dressed receptionist, who is made up to look more like a beautician than a medical receptionist.

Fortunately, Jenni has time in the waiting room to cool down and dry out before a nurse calls her name and ushers her into a small room with prominent scales against the wall. The nurse gets straight down to business, recording her height, weight, waist circumference and blood pressure.

The nurse then asks Jenni questions about her medical history. They're mostly questions Jenni has already answered, but she figures they need to double-check these things.

Jenni is then directed back to the waiting room to wait for the surgeon. She tries distracting herself, scrolling through Facebook, while she waits the fifteen minutes before her name is called again.

She looks up to see a clean-shaven man, hair styled with gel, wearing a suit with an open collar that makes his formal attire appear more casual. His smile is somewhat smug and knowing and Jenni can't tell if she sees compassion or judgement in his eyes. She follows him down a hallway and then he gestures for her to sit as they enter his spacious office. Jenni takes in the posters alongside one wall and a stomach model prominently positioned on his desk.

He sits and then gets straight to it. 'So, tell me Jenni, what brought you in today?'

Wow, that's pretty obvious, she thinks, but goes on to explain how she has struggled with her weight her entire life. She tells him about all the diets she's attempted and failed. He asks questions about her eating and exercise habits and her weight fluctuations. And she shares how she is fed up with her weight and is ready to make a change. Although he doesn't say much, she somehow feels validated by him.

The surgeon explains that 'diets don't work–as you're essentially starving yourself,' to which Jenni can relate. She nods as he continues to explain the problems with diets. 'The thing is, 95 per cent of people regain the weight they lose on a diet and often their weight increases with each diet attempt they fail. That is why, for someone like yourself, we recommend weight loss surgery, which is clinically proven to work.' So far, he is making sense to Jenni.

'In the majority of cases, people's struggle with weight is not their fault. Placing the blame on the individual does more to perpetuate shame and stigma than fix the problem.' He looks at her a moment, noticing the disbelief on her face. 'Obesity is a chronic non-curable life-threatening illness,' he asserts. 'It is a medical condition that is the cause of many health problems that can reduce the quality of life and life expectancy.'

Jenni isn't sure whether to feel comforted or overwhelmed by these words and the long list of associated health conditions he continues to list.

'We see surgery as a safe and effective means to obtain good health and increase life expectancy,' he concludes.

'But are there dangers with having surgery?' Jenni queries, still feeling nervous.

He confidently shakes his head to indicate no. 'Complications are rare,' he says. He then takes a deep breath and explains, 'Weight loss surgery is far safer than carrying around excess weight. The scientific evidence indicates that the complications from surgery far outweigh the life reduction caused by obesity.'

'Huh?' is all Jenni can manage.

'Maybe if I explain the various procedures?' he suggests, giving her an assuring smile.

Jenni nods for him to continue, and he explains in detail the procedures they specialise in at the clinic. 'There are various bariatric surgeries suitable for different cases, but it does come down to personal choice. In your case, your BMI is over 40, which means you are eligible for gastric bypass or gastric sleeve, which are the two procedures I'd recommend for you.'

As Dr Johnson explains the procedures step-by-step, pointing to the posters along the wall, Jenni feels more comfortable with this obviously compassionate and confident man. It makes absolute sense that if you reduce the size of your stomach, you will eat less. But also, there would be fewer receptors to send hunger signals to the brain. It sounds like an absolute godsend.

However, she has to fight back the butterflies in her stomach at the thought of having incisions into her abdomen and being put under a general anaesthetic. She hates hospitals and medical procedures. Some of her fear stems from the judgement she has felt in medical situations in the past. The thought of altering a part of her body that obviously plays an important role—digestion—causes her some nervousness.

She pushes her feelings of nervousness aside as the surgeon goes on to explain the pre-and post-operative procedure. It involves a liquid diet two weeks before and after surgery, followed by a purée diet and then a soft foods diet for a few weeks each. Then there is meal planning support for the first year after surgery, at which point she's likely to lose 70 per cent of her excess body weight. The thought of this sounds incredible to Jenni. Never in her life, with any diet she's ever tried, has she lost such a large amount of weight, and this was a sure thing—this was surgery.

By this stage of the consultation, Jenni feels confident, despite her nervousness, that surgery is the way to go. Fortunately, Dr Johnson clearly wants to proceed cautiously. He explains the process is something of a partnership, and it is necessary she commits to the surgery. He explains it will not only require her diligence for the twelve months post-surgery but ongoing for the rest of her life.

The commitment required sounds overwhelming, but the promise of so much weight loss is exhilarating. At that moment,

Jenni feels if she lost the weight, she'd do whatever it took to keep it off and look after her health going forward.

Yet, despite the certainty and excitement she feels, Jenni doesn't want to commit without taking some time to think it through and psych herself up to go under the knife. Dr Johnson graciously acknowledges it is a big decision and explains the payment options and pre-operative appointments required should she wish to proceed. He lets her know the current wait time and tells her to call the clinic when she is ready. He hands her a patient information booklet, paperwork and a sheet of costs before shaking her hand. She leaves his consultation room with a bounce in her step.

Although she hasn't signed any paperwork yet, Jenni somehow feels a sense of lightness. She feels a sense of freedom from her burdening weight.

And now, outside the weight loss clinic, Jenni no longer feels the same shame she did on arrival. She schedules an Uber right out front and smiles to herself the whole ride to work.

That evening Jenni reads the conditions of surgery document the surgeon provided her, along with the patient information booklet. She flips to the summary checklist at the end, where she is required to tick beside the conditions and then sign the document to confirm she's read it and agrees to the terms of conditions. She runs through the list:

1. "I will take a bariatric-specific multivitamin and calcium supplement for the rest of my life." *Sure*, she thinks.

2. "I will quit smoking two months before surgery and remain smoke-free for the rest of my life." *Easy, I never liked smoking, even those few months that I tried it in high school.* It had simply been a way to hang out with the 'cool' kids.

3. "I will follow up in the clinic after surgery at two weeks, three months, six months, 12 months and annually." *Okay, that's quite a commitment, but I can manage it.*

4. "I will follow the guidelines of the pre-and post-operative diet." At this, Jenni flips back to the section that outlines the dietary requirements. It looks just as regimented as any diet she's tried. *But it's worth it,* she thinks. She then notices the footnote that mentions that losing 10 per cent of body weight before surgery can reduce the risk of complications. *Phew, that's a big ask,* she thinks, considering her previous diet *success.* But she also suspects that anything to make the process as smooth as possible has got to be a good thing. So, although she's relieved it's not essential, and she is unlikely to achieve such dramatic weight loss before surgery, she notes that continuing to attempt to lose weight is worthwhile.

5. "I will not get pregnant for at least two years after my surgery." *Exceedingly unlikely,* she smirks to herself. Since Paul, she'd only ventured to the bedroom part of a date twice and neither had become a regular thing. No, the chance of becoming pregnant is negligible.

6. "I will exercise on a regular basis after surgery." *Yes,* she thinks, feeling again like she's signing off on a weight loss program.

Jenni scans through the document for a while before deciding to go online to find out more about the procedure and read patients' stories. On the Sunshine Weight Loss Solutions website, the before and after images are inspiring and Jenni begins to feel more confident with the idea of surgery. Apart from her aversion to medical procedures, she can't see any reason why not.

∽

The following day, Wednesday, Jenni walks into the lunchroom to pour herself a tea just as Norelle dunks a biscuit into her cuppa. *What is she doing?* Jenni wonders. *Not only has she given in to the temptation of those fundraising biscuits that scream "eat me", she's also eating them in plain sight, where anyone who walks by can see her indulgence.* Jenni would never—or at least avoid—sitting and eating her *guilty pleasures* where others could see her.

'Morning,' Norelle sings out.

'Good morning,' Jenni responds quickly, making her way back to her desk beside Pam.

Now Pam, on the other hand, she's Jenni's ally in the office. They've been working side-by-side for coming up to six years. Pam has been there for Jenni through many turbulent times, particularly as her relationship with Paul deteriorated and eventually ended. However, most notably, they are allies in their fight against weight.

Although the other female staff talk about *watching* what they eat, as most women do, Jenni and Pam are the only ones that could be described as large. Pam is a good two dress sizes smaller than Jenni, and her body would politely be described as plump. However, despite their size difference, Jenni feels that Pam, eight years her senior, knows what it is to battle your weight your entire life. Pam always has a sarcastic comment to make about eating or an excuse for spoiling themselves. She is one to always be breaking a diet and resolving to start another next week. It is Pam's constant concern with weight and eating that makes Jenni feel comfortable in sharing her personal struggles with her.

Leaning across her desk towards Pam, Jenni whispers with widening eyes. 'Have you met Norelle yet?'

'Briefly.' Pam gives a slight shrug.

'She's... quite an eccentric character.' Jenni looks for confirmation.

'She sure is.' Pam leans in, lowering her voice, 'Yesterday, I'm pretty sure she was meditating before she ate her lunch.'

'Well, right now, she's sitting in the lunchroom with tea and a biscuit.' Jenni nods toward the lunchroom. 'Who sits in there to have morning tea on their own?'

'I know. It's almost like she ceremoniously eats,' Pam says sharply.

'Well, you wouldn't catch me dead eating those fundraising biscuits,' Jenni states matter-of-factly.

'Me neither,' Pam enthusiastically agrees.

Jenni laughs as she turns back to her computer. She can always count on Pam to see things her way.

Pam and Jenni enjoy their unassuming position hidden away in the office. Except on Wednesdays, when Amanda joins them to support Pam with payroll. Amanda is of the opinion that all it takes is hard work to maintain a healthy weight, and she often tells them so. She clearly has no idea of how hard it is to lose weight and demotivating, not to mention demoralising, to starve yourself for weeks on end to have only a few grams budge. Thus, Pam and Jenni have a pact not to talk about food or weight concerns on Wednesdays.

So, rather than a day they discuss their eating, Wednesdays have become the day of the week they catch up on office gossip. Amanda always requests updates from the customer service ladies on everything that has transpired since her time in the office the week prior. Pam and Jenni generally receive updates inadvertently as they often overhear Amanda's conversations, or she can't contain herself when she returns to her desk.

On this Wednesday, Jenni can hear Amanda's shrill voice from the lunchroom as she catches up with Becca. 'A beach house!

That would be fantastic, Becca. You could work on your tan every weekend, and the kids could play at the beach.' There is a pause. 'Hey, and Adam could work on the up-keep of that body of his.'

Becca, never one to blush at a compliment, continues, 'I hope we find something we love.'

'You will. You can get anything you put your mind to, Becca,' Amanda says before making a beeline to her desk beside Pam.

Jenni feels like puking. *Of course, Becca can get anything she puts her mind to. She's fucking gorgeous.*

Unlike Amanda and Becca, nothing feels easy for Jenni. Nor achievable, no matter how much she puts her mind to it. She doesn't have the perfect body. The perfect husband. The perfect children. And although she resents Becca in so many ways, she also envies the ease with which she moves through the world.

Jenni's thought, that Becca can get anything she puts her mind to, causes her to start thinking about the surgery and whether she should go ahead with it. *If Becca were fat, she would do it; she'd take control of her life,* Jenni contemplates.

Later that day, when Pam gets back from a toilet break, Jenni rolls her chair over to Pam's desk and whispers, 'I didn't know if I wanted to tell you. Actually, anyone for that matter. Yesterday... I... I had an appointment with a weight loss surgeon.' Jenni cringes in expectation of Pam's reaction.

'What?... Wow!... Really?' Pam exclaims and then continues flatly, 'Brian would never let me do that.'

Jenni is unsure why Pam's remark immediately went to Brian rather than enquiring about the surgery. Thinking that Pam's comment may have been regarding safety, Jenni explains, 'It's... it's much safer than it used to be and there are a variety of procedures they do depending on how much weight you need to lose.'

Unfortunately, Amanda, sitting on the other side of the divider to Pam, overhears this and leans round. 'Are you trying another diet, Jenni?' she asks.

Pam glances to Jenni, waiting for a response. Jenni doesn't want Amanda gossiping about something that she hasn't yet decided whether she'll go ahead with. So, she responds, 'I'm thinking about it.'

'I think that's great, Jenni,' Amanda says, turning back to her desk.

Jenni rolls her eyes and mouths to Pam, 'Later.'

Neither the reaction from Pam nor the comment from Amanda makes Jenni feel any better about herself. *What fucking business is it of anyone whether I'm going to lose weight, anyway,* Jenni thinks as she gets back to her work, wishing she'd never mentioned it. It is a decision she has to make for herself.

Chapter 3

"Right now, you weigh what you weigh, and no amount of thinking otherwise, resisting it, self-reprimanding, punishing yourself, guilt or shame is going to change your weight or health right now."

— Joyful Eating

The following week, in their weekly staff meeting before the glass doors open to the public, Norelle gives a short presentation covering the projects and initiatives she'll be working on. In addition to her involvement in tree planting, book fairs and mural painting, she'll be working on a collaborative project with the City Council putting together a festival. Something of an arts and careers festival showcasing local writers, artists and performers, where families can get involved in activities and games to tap into their creativity and imagination. Jenni admits to herself that it does sound like a good initiative and Norelle is definitely the right person for the job. With qualifications in economics, a degree she admits she attained as it was considered the sensible thing to do, Norelle seems suitably placed in a role that requires creativity and relatability.

After the presentation, with ten minutes to spare before opening time, the staff mill around sipping tea and coffee. Pam heads over to Norelle to enquire about the schools that the Union is working with while Jenni stands back, sipping her tea.

On the other side of the meeting room, Jenni notices Becca is beaming with excitement as she declares to the customer service ladies, Mora and Rachel, that she and Adam have found their dream beach house up on the Sunshine Coast.

Rachel shrieks. 'Wow, that is amazing! You only started looking last week.'

Mora squeals with excitement. 'You should have a beach house… house warming party!'

'Oh, yes, that would be fabulous,' Rachel agrees as everyone's eyes turn to Becca, offering her congratulations.

'Well… Asher's fifth birthday is coming up,' Becca muses. 'We could have a combined party,' she says, flicking her long, luscious locks of hair behind one shoulder.

'Ooh, you could have a themed party…' Jenni hears Rachel's screeching voice continue.

And so, the conversation carries on. Now, with everyone, including Pam and Priya, engrossed in the conversation. All eyes are on Becca, as always. All except for Norelle and Barry, who talk quietly beside the table where she has her laptop set up. Jenni now finds herself on the outside of the conversation, standing against the glass wall.

She feels conspicuous standing there, left out from the conversation. She cares and doesn't care all at the same time. She can't imagine anything worse than hanging out with her colleagues in swimwear, but feels a slight wave of dejection that the others wouldn't involve her in the conversation. She decides to retreat to her desk.

When Pam returns and takes a seat, Jenni whispers, 'Can you imagine anything worse than a beach party—everyone frolicking around in bikinis?'

'Heck, no,' Pam agrees, 'I was just listening out of morbid curiosity.'

'Thankfully, I escaped that conversation,' Jenni concludes. Although truthfully, she resents it. She resents that the others didn't even consider including her in the conversation. She resents all the times she seems invisible to others—all the times people haven't considered inviting or including her in their plans.

Yet, despite how much she despises being invisible, she knows it's a far sight better than being conspicuous—of standing out because of her body. Jenni slipped away from the conversation as she knows that standing out hurts more than missing out.

Jenni was seven years old when she first became aware her body was a *problem*. Her family had spent the morning at the beach, swimming and building sandcastles. She had moved and played freely without any self-consciousness.

Then, during the afternoon, her mother brought ice creams down to where Jenni and her sister were playing. Jenni ripped at the packaging with excitement and poked the top into her mouth, sucking hard on the chocolate coating. She grinned up at her father, who was looking at her with dismay.

He shook his head. 'You'll have to stop eating like that if you want to have a *healthy figure*, Jen-Jen,' he'd said. At the time, it didn't mean much, but it was imprinted on her subconscious: she had to eat a certain way to maintain a healthy figure—whatever that was.

From then on, Jenni's father would make off-hand remarks about how much she ate. He regularly told her she'd have to watch what she ate if she wanted to be slim like her mother and sister. Yet her sister would enjoy ice creams and treats as Jenni did, and he never commented on her eating.

By twelve, Jenni had learnt to hide her eating from her father. If her mother bought her a treat, she'd save it for later and eat it in her room. She'd show utter constraint in front of her father. However, when she got to her bedroom, she would devour her stash.

By fifteen, Jenni could purchase treats for herself and keep them hidden away. She would eat a small meal at the dinner table to please her father and then snack on salted nuts, chips and chocolate in her room while she studied or read.

She learned to do the same at school to avoid other kids' judgment, who would sneer at Jenni if they saw her eating, despite eating chips and pies themselves.

Jenni ate alone to protect herself. However, she could become so hungry that by the time she got to her bedroom, she'd eat food by the handful, shoving it into her mouth and gulping it down.

℃

'Are either of you hungry?' Norelle's voice chirps as she walks into Jenni and Pam's office around midday.

Jenni's been hungry for as long as she can remember. 'I sure am,' she declares, 'however, I'm going to stick to a diet shake at my desk.'

'Me too.' Pam shrugs. 'We're watching our weight.'

'Oh, okay. I hope that is enough to satisfy you.' Norelle nods to the shakers on their desks.

Satisfy us! Jenni thinks. *As if a shake could ever be a satisfying meal.* 'Not really. But it's what we have to do in the name of health,' Jenni responds, grimacing.

Norelle shakes her head empathetically. 'I don't believe that dieting is necessary for good health.'

'Well, what other way is there?' Pam asks incredulously.

'I believe in slowing down and tuning in to nourish my body

in a way that makes me feel most energetic and alive. I used to be obsessed with my weight and diet. However, I've come to a place where my eating is more intuitive,' Norelle explains.

Pam laughs and shoots Jenni a smile. 'I'm not sure I could trust the intuitive messages my body sends me.'

However, Jenni doesn't laugh. 'How can you trust your body to tell you what and how much to eat?'

'It took time, and it wasn't easy. I had to learn to distinguish my body's hunger and fullness signals from the diet and food rules ingrained in my mind my entire life. But I started by learning to eat consciously. And then I explored my beliefs one by one, which were holding me in a pattern of yo-yo dieting.'

Pam still has her mind on the dieting aspect of the conversation and states in a questioning way, 'I can't believe you ever needed to diet, Norelle.'

'Oh, I fought five to ten kilos for much of my twenties and thirties, like many other women. However, all it did was keep me in a cycle of dieting and body dissatisfaction. Now, I care for my body in a more respectful and intuitive way.'

Although Jenni has considerably more than five kilos to lose, she is curious. 'So, you mean that mindful eating or whatever you call it helped you stop dieting?'

'That, among some other practices, yes,' Norelle confirms, 'I've come to realise that it's not control over our bodies and eating we require, but an awareness and acceptance of it.'

'Sounds great, but I'm not sure it would be a suitable approach for those of us who have a lot of weight to lose,' Pam protests.

'The thing is, it isn't about weight loss. It's about health and caring for the body you have, no matter your size,' Norelle explains, 'we are so obsessed with weight loss that we forget what truly matters: health and happiness.'

Norelle certainly seems to be a cheerful person, uninhibited by others' opinions of her. Jenni is intrigued. Ignoring Pam's sceptical look, Jenni looks to Norelle. 'I'd love to learn more about this intuitive eating stuff sometime.'

Norelle enthusiastically responds in a warm tone, 'Sure thing.' Then goes to leave.

'Enjoy your lunch,' Jenni calls almost on autopilot as you do when being polite.

However, Norelle's response is not the usual 'thanks,' but a convincing, 'I most definitely will.'

When Jenni sips on her diet shake, she envisages Norelle out somewhere, eating her lunch in her usual meditative way.

As Jenni walks home, she feels as hungry as she does most evenings. She is so hungry that the idea of preparing food seems impossible and only a delay in filling the void she feels.

As she opens a bag of potato chips and turns on the TV, Jenni reflects on the conversation with Norelle. Could there be an easier way than all the struggle? Could she break out of this restrict-binge-restrict cycle and daintily eat one biscuit? Should she explore Norelle's approach to food before committing to surgery?

There is only one way to find out.

The thought of having her stomach stapled gives her shivers. If she could lose weight another way, she'd save herself the time off work, the expense and a procedure that gave her the heebie-jeebies. *There's no harm delaying it a little longer*, she assures herself.

The next day Jenni keeps her eye on the glass meeting rooms, eager to talk with Norelle. She notices Barry looking as smart as ever, working on his computer. He waves in her direction. Mortified, Jenni keeps her head down and a less obvious eye on the offices.

When Norelle arrives close to closing, the knees of her denim jeans covered in dirt, Jenni makes her way over to the glass room. 'Norelle?'

'Oh. Hi Jenni,' Norelle smiles, looking up from her laptop.

'Norelle. I've been wondering, could you tell me more about this intuition and eating stuff you were talking about yesterday?'

'Sure. I've just got to send a few emails to report on today's tree planting. But we could go out for a cuppa after work if you like?' Norelle suggests.

'Really?... You sure?' Jenni is surprised Norelle can meet with her straightaway. *Doesn't she have an art class or a bird-watching group to go to?*

'Absolutely.' Norelle smiles. 'It's no problem. It will be lovely to chat with you—I know just the place.' Her smile seems to grow even broader.

'Uh... great! Works for me.' Jenni still feels somewhat caught off guard that Norelle can make the time for her right away.

'I'll come by when I'm done here.' Norelle nods toward her laptop.

'Brilliant.' Jenni feels a light skip to her step as she makes her way back to her desk.

Chapter 4

"Acceptance of your body doesn't mean that you necessarily love your body, but that you no longer fight against it."

—Joyful Eating

❧

Jenni stands in line beside Norelle. She tries to avoid looking at the array of chocolates on display. *She's taken me to a fucking chocolate shop to talk to me about my diet!* Jenni thinks with confusion. Norelle, on the other hand, inspects the chocolates closely—her head lowered to the cabinet-level.

Jenni tries to pay no attention to Norelle. *She's taken me to the fucking lion's den,* Jenni thinks. *She's going to sit in this place, right in front of me and nibble on chocolate while I have to employ every restraint not to eat everything in the café. It better be bloody good coffee here!*

Yet, the smell of chocolate is irresistible—this will be a test of Jenni's willpower to resist. She's going to have to employ every ounce of self-control to ignore the chocolate all around her: in the cabinet, on the shelves, on the wallpaper, on the napkins.

Norelle interrupts Jenni's thoughts. 'Have you decided what you'd like?'

'Oh… it all looks so delicious… but I… I really shouldn't… I'm going to stick to a coffee,' Jenni says, forcing a smile.

'Okay,' Norelle says, unfazed by Jenni's refusal of chocolate, 'I'm going to have a chocolate with my coffee.'

'There is no way I could eat just one chocolate,' Jenni ponders aloud. 'Once I eat one, then I'd be away; there'd be no stopping me. I'd eat everything. And I don't mean here. I'd likely eat chocolate or whatever I could get my hands on when I get home. Once I start, it's hard to stop. There is absolutely no way I could stick to one chocolate.'

'Why do you think that is?' Norelle asks.

'Chocolate is irresistible,' Jenni states.

'Yes, chocolate is scrumptious. But why do you think you can't enjoy the deliciousness of one mouthful or one chocolate?'

'I don't know… I'm greedy. I've got no self-control.' Jenni shrugs.

'I don't think it's more control that you require,' Norelle says tenderly. 'No, it's greater awareness of the experience of eating chocolate, without the thoughts in your mind that tell you that you should or should not be eating what you're eating. The thoughts that tell you that once you start eating, you may as well keep going as you've blown it today.'

Jenni knows she struggles to stop once she starts eating, but is unconvinced by what Norelle says. 'I don't know… if I stopped trying to control my eating, wouldn't it spiral completely out of control? Would the eating ever stop?'

'Would you like to find out?' Norelle gives an encouraging smile.

'No, not really. The end result wouldn't be pretty.' Jenni is pretty sure, given past experience, how it would go.

'So,' Norelle says gently, 'you're saying that you know what would happen if you released the reins of control over your eating?'

'Of course. I'd eat everything I wanted.'

Yet Norelle isn't done with her questions. 'And do you know what you want?'

'Well, everything that tastes good,' Jenni returns matter-of-factly.

'But is that all you want from life?'

Jenni squirms, feeling uncomfortable with the question: what does she want from life? She shrugs. 'Um, food is one of life's pleasures?' she says, not sure that's the answer Norelle's looking for.

'It sure is,' Norelle affirms, 'but it isn't life's only pleasure.'

Just then, their attention is drawn away from one another as the lady in front of them pays for her order. It allows them both a moment to pause from their conversation, which has suddenly become intense.

Jenni isn't sure where this conversation is going and whether she really wants to be here anymore. Not only does she have to contend with the temptation of chocolate, but she has to face some hard truths: what does she want from life? Chocolate? Food? Or are these only distractions that preclude her from having to face her true desires and the reality that she has no idea what she wants?

Norelle places her hand on Jenni's forearm. 'Jenni... I understand that it can be hard to quieten your inner critic that attempts to control your eating. However, it is that voice that creates the suffering, not the pleasure of food.'

Jenni glances at Norelle. *Did she just read my mind? Is she a psychic or something?*

'Shall we?' Norelle motions to the counter.

'What can I get you today?' the café attendant asks Norelle.

'I'd love a short black and a dark chocolate praline.' Norelle glances at Jenni. 'I love the contrast of the bitter coffee to the sweetness of the chocolate.' She is the epitome of a child in a lolly shop, unafraid to hide her joy.

Norelle pays for her order, and the café attendant then looks to Jenni. 'And how about you?'

'Um, it's all so tempting. But I'll stick to a skinny caramel latté,' Jenni answers.

As the EFTPOS receipt whirs out, the café attendant presents Norelle and Jenni with a small tray of chocolate chips. 'Ladies, would you like to sample our new salted caramel dark chocolate bark?'

Jenni hesitates while Norelle gleams. 'We most definitely would. Though, rather than have it here, would you mind putting it on a saucer so we can enjoy it at our table?'

The café attendant obliges and hands Norelle a saucer with three tiny pieces of chocolate.

'Thanks, we'll savour these,' Norelle says. *What the hell?!* Jenni thinks. *Those shards of chocolate are what's left in the bottom of a chocolate wrapper after I've devoured the entire bar. Savour it! Why wouldn't she pop them straight into her mouth at the counter, like a normal person?* Despite a sense of frustration, Jenni is intrigued by Norelle. *Where did she get this self-control?*

They make their way to a table by the window overlooking a leafy garden. Norelle places the saucer with the three shards of chocolate on the table as they seat themselves.

They sit there a moment, Norelle's eyes on the chocolate shards, while Jenni tries her best to ignore them.

'These pieces of chocolate provide us with a good opportunity, Jenni,' Norelle proposes.

'How's that?' Jenni asks incredulously.

'We can practice eating with our full awareness, tuning into our senses, not the thoughts in our mind that tell us what we should or should not be eating,' Norelle explains.

'Oh, okay,' Jenni says, trying to hide her scepticism.

Norelle begins to explain. 'This practice is what I like to call conscious eating. It is eating with our full awareness of the sensory experience of eating; how it looks, smells, sounds, tastes and feels, without judgement or an internal commentary as to what we should or should not be eating.'

Jenni nods as Norelle continues, 'So often, people eat distracted or mindlessly. It may be because they're busy or don't feel they deserve the pleasure of food. They may deprive themselves of the joy of truly experiencing what they're eating due to guilt and shame. And unfortunately, mindless eating can cause them to think they can't control themselves around food or that they eat too much.'

Norelle looks at Jenni knowingly. Jenni makes no move to say anything as she's taking in Norelle's words.

'Shall we give it a try?' Norelle continues without waiting for Jenni's confirmation. 'First, we look at what we are about to eat. This is why it is good to place it on a plate or in a bowl rather than eating directly out of a package. We observe the colour, shape and texture of the food. We acknowledge whether it looks appealing and whether or not we really want it.'

Jenni sits mesmerised by the tiny chocolate shards on the saucer. She examines the thin, dark, glossy chocolate haphazardly crisscrossed with raised threadlike strands of shiny caramel, which is contrasted by glistening flakes of white salt.

'Next, we bring the chocolate to our nose and take in its aroma. You can pick up the plate.' Norelle motions to Jenni.

Jenni picks up the saucer and brings it to her nose. She closes her eyes and takes in a deep breath, allowing the volatile chocolate molecules to enter her nostrils and touch the back of her throat. Despite the overwhelming chocolate aroma in the café, the smell of this dark chocolate is intense. She smells the nuttiness of the chocolate and the sweet buttery caramel. She feels deeply relaxed. She opens her eyes and places the saucer on the table.

Norelle smiles at her. 'Next, we take a piece and feel it between our fingers, noticing the texture. Then, as you take a bite, notice the texture and flavour.'

Jenni takes a shard of chocolate between her fingers. She notices its firm but smooth texture, the stickiness of the caramel and the grittiness of the salt sprinkled on top. She feels it soften with the warmth of her fingers.

She then brings it to her mouth, taking in the aroma before placing it on her tongue.

She hears and feels the snap of the chocolate as she bites into it. She notices the taste of salt as it touches the roof of her mouth. Then, as she crushes it between her teeth, she discerns the rich bitterness of the chocolate against the sweet and salty flavours of the threaded caramel and salt crystals. As it melts in her mouth, she feels its silky smoothness on her tongue. She moves it around her mouth until it fully melts and all the flavours combine.

She swallows, noticing the flavours and sensations that linger in her mouth. 'Oh, that's delicious.'

'It sure is,' Norelle says, taking a piece of chocolate herself.

Jenni watches Norelle eat the chocolate and contemplates how much slower and more mindful this way of eating is, how you can experience so much pleasure from such a small piece of chocolate. It is as if less is more when you're conscious that you're eating.

'I can really see how eating this way can help you eat less,' Jenni muses.

'Yet, that is not the intent,' Norelle clarifies, 'the intention is to be fully aware of the experience of eating—how it feels in your body—and to eat exactly what and how much feels good to your body. It may mean eating more or less, but the focus is not to modify your intake, but to tune in.' She pauses. 'So, how did it taste?'

'Sensational.' Jenni beams, pleasantly surprised.

Norelle enquires further, 'And how do you feel?'

'I feel an immense sense of satisfaction.' Jenni considers the question further. 'I feel like I really enjoyed everything that little piece of chocolate had to give.'

'The chocolate provides pleasure, but the joy of eating it, that came from within you,' Norelle confirms. Her eyes look directly into Jenni's. 'You brought joy to the experience by eating it with your full awareness.'

The café attendant arrives with their coffees and Norelle's praline, breaking their contemplative eye contact. Jenni looks at her skinny caramel latté and then brings it to her nose. She takes in the aroma of the coffee and caramel before taking a sip. She allows it to linger in her mouth—to fully taste the flavour and sensations before swallowing. It is sweet and creamy with the underlying acidity of coffee. She places her latté glass back on its saucer.

After a few more sips, Jenni feels a warmth within her torso. She feels the sweet taste overpowering the coffee. She places the glass on the saucer again. But this time pushes it aside as she continues to talk with Norelle. She feels like she is fully present with the conversation and intently listens as Norelle tells her about her latest gardening project at a local school, a garden to plate initiative.

When they stand to leave, Jenni comments to Norelle, 'You know, that's the first time I've realised how sweet caramel lattés are? Normally, I'd keep drinking because I've bought it and it is there. Today, I realised I didn't want it. Look at it, cold with a milk skin. It couldn't look any more unappealing, could it?'

Norelle smiles.

It dawns on Jenni that this is the difference between awareness and control.

⸎

That evening on the train home, Jenni decides to pick up a few things for her dinner to practice conscious eating. She buys a hummus dip, carrots, grapes, a block of Gouda cheese and a packet of crackers.

Once home, she slices the carrot and a few pieces of cheese, placing them on a plate with a small bunch of grapes and a few crackers. However, rather than plop herself in front of the TV, she sits at her dining table, which is a bit of a mission, as she has to push the scattered papers and books aside. She can't remember the last time she's eaten at the table and makes a mental note to tidy up, so it is more enticing.

She sits and contemplates her plate. It is so quiet in her apartment—just her and this plate of food. She stands to open a window to let in a light breeze and then turns her chair side on so the clutter at the other end of the table is no longer distracting. *Here we go*, she thinks as she begins.

She picks up one carrot stick and takes a bite, noticing the loudness as she crunches into it. She feels her jaw moving as the firmness becomes soft and the sweetness of the carrot releases in her mouth. *Have carrots always tasted this good?*

Next, she dips a carrot stick into the hummus. In contrast to the carrot on its own, the hummus' garlic flavour is intense but mellows as she chews.

She continues to consciously eat the items on her plate, but begins to feel this is taking some time. She feels an overwhelming need to do something else, anything to distract her from eating. She has to consciously bring herself back to her eating and fight the temptation to reach for her phone or read one of the documents on her table. She realises how impulsive it is to distract herself while she eats.

She continues to eat, switching between the cheese's rich creaminess and the carrot's fresh crunchiness. Then a burst of the sweetness of the grapes and the dry saltiness of the crackers. She notices how they complement each other, which is obvious on the one hand, but not something she's ever really contemplated.

Although it is somewhat challenging, she finds the experience incredibly satisfying—she relishes the foods on the plate and feels sufficiently satiated.

Packing away a few remaining grapes and cheese, Jenni decides to make a cup of herbal tea to sip while watching TV. As she waits for the kettle to boil, she notices she feels satisfied but not overly full. She fights the urge to think how this will help her to lose weight, as Norelle had been adamant that was not the intent. However, the idea of taking an approach other than dieting and surgery sure is appealing, especially since she isn't sure she can face the scalpel.

Jenni makes a mental note to ask Norelle to explain why she shouldn't use this conscious eating practice as a way to gain control of her weight. However, it is evident how much more enjoyable this approach to eating is than her usual stuff it in and then feel immense guilt and shame afterwards.

'Morning,' Jenni says as she places her handbag under her desk.

Pam looks up from her computer screen. 'Morning, Jenni.' Then, hesitantly and almost cringing, she asks, 'How did your afternoon catch up with Norelle go?'

'Actually, it was pretty... great!' Jenni admits. She continues with enthusiasm, 'We actually enjoyed a coffee and chocolate together!'

'Chocolate?' Pam gives an expression that reflects her unspoken words, *Are you kidding me?*

'I know! It was unnerving. However, Norelle really helped me see that I don't have to eat the entire chocolate display to satisfy my hunger and cravings.' Jenni shoots Pam a grin. 'Afterwards, I even went home and made a snack plate with cheese, crackers and carrots—I forgot how good raw carrot tastes.'

'Oh, that sounds so simple. Easier for you, though... on your own. Brian expects a decent meal every night and definitely no rabbit food.'

At least you have someone to enjoy a meal with, Jenni thinks, although she'd never say anything like that out loud, especially not to Pam. However, sometimes it does feel like people complain about what they have and forget that others don't have those things. Not that Jenni is in any rush for a relationship, but sometimes it feels too quiet all alone in her apartment.

⁓

'Afternoon,' Norelle calls as Jenni turns off her computer for the day.

'Afternoon,' Jenni repeats, collecting her handbag.

Norelle begins to rummage through some boxes on the shelf by the photocopier. Then explains, 'I've got to get some merchandise for the book fair tomorrow. I remember seeing some calculators somewhere.'

'Yep, there's a bunch in the blue box.' Jenni gestures to the top shelf. 'Is there anything else you need? We've got notepads. They could work for a book fair?'

'Oh, yes, that might be better than calculators—encourage young writers and all that.' Norelle smiles.

Jenni pulls out the bottom drawer of Amanda's desk, which contains dozens of packets containing notepads. 'Perfect,' Norelle declares, 'you're a lifesaver. I can't believe I left this to the last minute. I'm still getting the hang of this position.'

'No worries. How many do you think you'll need?'

'Um... I'll take forty, then see how many I give away. Is it okay to submit the paperwork tomorrow when I get back?'

'That's fine. We'll just note how many you take so that you can accurately record how many you give away. We'd better get the figures right for Priya.' Jenni gives Norelle a look that says, *be cautious.*

'Oh, okay. Thanks for helping me with this, Jenni.'

'All good. Thanks for taking the time with me yesterday.'

'Have you practised conscious eating since?' Norelle asks.

'I sure did.' Jenni smiles. 'Actually, I forgot how much I enjoy the taste of raw carrots—they are so crunchy and sweet. I think I've avoided eating them raw because I've associated them with diet food for so long.'

'That's the thing. The intent of conscious eating is to engage all the senses while getting out of our heads as to what is good or bad or what we should or should not be eating. We can then eat carrots without thinking of them as healthy. We can simply enjoy them.'

'I can see that,' Jenni confirms.

'Was there anything that you found challenging?'

Jenni ponders the question a moment. 'I think the quietness and feeling it was just me and the food. It was a little unnerving.'

'Yes, we're so used to noise and distraction that it can be hard to cope with silence,' Norelle agrees.

'Sure, but most people have someone to eat with and talk to.' Jenni feels like she's beginning to sound like she's whining. *Oh damn, maybe Pam's rubbing off on me.*

'Yes, it can be enjoyable to eat with others. However, if the desire is to distract, it's not the right reason,' Norelle clarifies.

Jenni sighs despondently. 'I suppose it is something that I need to get used to. I'm probably destined to be alone for the rest of my life.'

'What... what do you mean?' Norelle looks somewhat bewildered. 'Why do you say that?'

'Well, look at me,' Jenni states. *Oh damn, I'm really whining now.*

'Jenni, how you look doesn't make you lovable. Your body does not define you or represent who you are. I get that society places considerable emphasis on appearance. However, it is not who you are.'

'Don't judge a book by its cover and all that,' Jenni agrees half-heartedly.

'Somewhat,' Norelle says, pausing to collect her thoughts. She continues. 'People judge one another all the time, for all sorts of reasons. Whether it be their body, their clothes, car, job, partner and so on. Unfortunately, you can't change that. So, concerning yourself with others' perception of you is a waste of time. The only thing you should concern yourself with is how you hold yourself back from being yourself and sharing what you have to offer the world for fear of others' judgement.'

Jenni's train of thought doesn't really shift with Norelle's words. 'I don't know. I just feel that I'm destined to be alone.'

'And you think that losing weight is the answer?' Norelle presses empathetically.

'Well…,' Jenni ponders.

'Do you truly believe that you would be more loveable if you lost weight?'

'Well, it would give someone the opportunity to move past *this*.' Jenni gestures to her body.

Norelle shakes her head slowly and gently replies, 'Unfortunately, losing weight provides no guarantee of finding love, Jenni.'

'I… I suppose not.' Jenni reflects on the many slim women she knows who are still, or were for a long time, single.

'Anyone who can't see past the exterior is not worthy of you, my dear.' Norelle insists.

Jenni decides not to push back any longer—*everyone is entitled to their own opinions,* she thinks. She nods without saying a word and Norelle gives a gentle, if not slightly sympathetic, smile.

∾

Jenni arrives home in a slightly deflated mood, Norelle's words still swirling around in her mind. The entire train ride home, she wonders if there is some truth to what Norelle had said, "losing weight provides no guarantee of finding love." Is that what she is looking for, love? She doesn't think so. Paul had loved her, hadn't he? And that still hadn't been enough.

Confused and slightly annoyed at herself as much as with Norelle, Jenni finishes off the carrot, crackers and cheese from the previous night while sitting in front of the TV. She then removes a tub of cookie dough ice cream from the freezer. Since all her bowls are still dirty in the dishwasher from the morning and previous evening, she decides to eat straight from the container. *It's still conscious eating if you can see it, right?*

However, as she eats, she starts to feel bad about what she's doing. She gobbles a few more spoonfuls as she puts the lid back on and returns it to the freezer. She realises she is eating only because of her foul mood, not hunger. Maybe Norelle is rubbing off on her after all?

∾

The next day, after midday, Jenni realises she's forgotten her lunch—her shake—so she decides to eat at the café downstairs. She doesn't like eating alone in cafés, but it's better than eating in front of everyone in the office lunchroom.

She orders a chicken pie and salad, the yin and yang on the healthy food spectrum and sits at a long table against the window. That way, she won't have to sit across from anyone as she eats.

She takes a bite of her pie and then remembers to tune into her senses. She notices the crunch and crispiness of the flaky crust contrasted against the soft, creamy, chewy centre. She chews slowly, noticing the flavours.

She's then taken out of the moment when she hears a familiar voice and realises he's speaking to her. 'Do you mind if I sit here?'

Jenni looks up to see Barry from Loans holding a plate supporting a loaded sandwich. *What is he doing here*? The last thing she wants is someone from the office seeing her eating. Although... it is inevitable, given the café is directly downstairs.

'Sure...,' she says. What else could she say?

'It's nice to get out of the office,' Barry comments.

'Uh-huh,' Jenni responds, shifting her knees to point away from the side he sits. She takes a forkful of salad.

'Do you come down here often?' he asks, 'it's just I haven't seen you in here before. And I have my lunch here most days.'

No, because everything is a thousand calories more than I can normally eat, she thinks. 'No, not really. I normally bring my own lunch.' *Diet shakes, that is*, she corrects herself.

'Wow, you must be prepared. I struggle to get to work on time, let alone get organised enough to make a healthy lunch.'

Oh, I didn't say it was healthy, she thinks as she throws him a smile.

Barry continues, 'I often get swept away with reading in the morning and completely forget what the time is.'

'Oh... reading?'

'I know, kinda nerdy, heh?'

'I didn't say anything.' She throws up her hands in a cheeky defence and shifts slightly toward him. 'So, tell me, what is it you enjoy reading so much?'

'I'm fascinated with anything medieval. I read historical novels set in that period.' He stops, and Jenni nods, urging him to continue. 'Life was so different than now—it's hard to comprehend. I don't know... life was much simpler, yet so much harsher. Just to survive was a challenge—even to put food on the table. Our generation has got it a lot easier.' Barry smiles at Jenni to gauge whether she agrees.

'Yep, get our pay and head to the supermarket with the only fear being that you'll get run over in the car park on the way in. Or maybe heartburn from eating too much steak.' She grins.

Barry laughs. 'Yeh, modern life is easier, but it doesn't have that much of an edge of excitement. I think that's why I'm so fascinated with the time period.'

Jenni remains silent, wondering what to say next. Barry continues, 'I want to travel and see other parts of the world. I was so focused on getting an education and getting into the housing market that I forgot to see the world. I'd love to go to Rome and visit the medieval castles. There is so much history there, compared to what we have in Australia.' He pauses. 'Have you been to Italy?'

God, no, she thinks. Although she'd love to go, she's always been fearful of travelling to places renowned for their food. She's always thought she'd travel when she no longer had to watch her weight. Thus, travel had never eventuated.

Despite her thoughts, Barry keeps talking, and before she knows it, they're having an enjoyable conversation. However, she can't help but wonder, *is he just trying to be nice because we work in the same office? Could he be interested in me? No. No, I can't think this way, only to discover that I've misread the signs. I really don't need any further disappointment in my life right now.*

She shakes off the fantasy—she can't let her mind go there. She has to stop this thinking right now to protect herself from further disappointment and heartbreak. She decides it's best to retreat.

Jenni interrupts him mid-sentence. 'I'm really sorry, Barry. It's been nice chatting, but I'd better get back.' She motions in the direction of the offices.

'But you haven't finished your lunch?' Barry protests with a look of confusion on his face.

'Oh, I didn't give myself enough time to eat and I don't want to intrude on your lunch.'

'Hey, you're not intruding. I intruded on your lunch! I can leave and find another space to sit if you like.' He glances around the packed café and then catches Jenni's eye.

'It's okay,' she says.

Why is he here? He only sat with me because it was the only space available. He only asked me to stay to be polite. Barry is a nice guy that could charm anyone. 'I really do have to get back,' she says, standing and positioning her handbag strap on her shoulder.

'Some other time, then,' he says in a way that is part statement and part question.

'Yep,' she says, walking away without a glance back. *Some other time? Some other time, what? Some other time, they'd talk, have lunch? No wonder the clients thought he was charming, making a girl feel like he's interested in her, which he couldn't possibly be.*

Anyway, Jenni isn't interested in a relationship with anyone; not until she loses her weight, not until she is her true self again. She doesn't want another relationship like she'd had with Paul, where he'd coddled her and assured her that her weight wasn't an issue when it clearly was.

As Jenni walks back to the office, she glances at her reflection in the double glass doors. *Men like Barry, they wouldn't even see a woman like me. Not in a romantic way,* she thinks. How can they see past this exterior that hides who she is deep down?

As she takes in her reflection, Jenni resolves that she will now, once and for all, lose her excess weight one way or another. She has to; for herself and to show the world who she could be. And she is onto a great start, only having had two bites of that creamy chicken pie. Surgery is looking like a good option at this point.

❧

Back at the office, Jenni makes herself a herbal tea to ward off the hunger pangs and heads back to her desk. She's 20 minutes early from her lunch break, so decides to devise a meal plan for the next week or so until she overcomes her fear and commits to undergoing surgery. She mightn't be able to lose ten per cent of her weight before going under the knife, but she could try to reduce the risk of complications. And she knows what she has to do to lose weight, why she's been on-again-off-again diets for over twenty years. So, she devises a plan.

Breakfast: skip it.

Morning: coffee.

Lunch: diet shake at her desk.

Dinner: chicken or fish with greens, like prescribed on the program she'd tried last year. She knew it was bland, but she knew the portions. She can do this. She would do this. She had to do this. If not now, when?

Jenni gets up to make another tea. The previous had barely hit her sides.

She is halfway to the urn before she realises Norelle is sitting there in the lunchroom, eating quietly. Jenni isn't in the mood to talk about conscious eating right now. She continues to the urn and then glances over her shoulder in Norelle's direction. 'Lovely day,' she says, turning to pull the lever to avoid eye contact.

'Sure is,' Norelle chirps, 'I was out this morning with a group of kids in their school garden. It was a gorgeous day for it!'

Norelle is all sunshine and colourful murals, as usual, Jenni thinks as she watches the water trickle over her teabag.

'Sounds great,' Jenni says, quickly turning for the door. 'I'd better get back to it—the reconciliation report won't make it to Priya's desk on its own.'

'Sure thing,' Norelle replies, contently contemplating the colourful contents of her lunchbox. *There she goes again, consciously eating her lunch, always perfectly present in her perfectly healthy body. She's got no fucking idea,* Jenni fumes to herself.

Jenni sits at her desk just as Barry makes his way to one of the glass meeting rooms. He waves. *Whatever,* she thinks, giving him a half-hearted nod.

℧

That evening when Jenni gets home, she is famished but prepared. She'd stopped in at the supermarket and now has an ample supply of zucchini, broccoli, green beans, spinach, salmon and chicken.

She weighs out 100 g of salmon and pops it under the grill. She then puts some broccoli on to steam. Once cooked, she plates them up and sits on the couch to watch sitcoms. She enjoys watching them, not because they're particularly funny, but they distract her from how boring her meal is. Before the ad break, her plate is empty.

Her weeknights continue this way, alternating between fish and chicken with the selection of vegetables she's purchased. It is easiest to keep it simple like this because if she mixes things with sauces and dressings, it is too hard to monitor her caloric intake. She is sticking to her new plan and she will do so until she sees the surgeon.

On the fourth night, to distract herself from her ever-increasing hunger, Jenni sorts her wardrobe... pulling out a selection of summery dresses she no longer fits into; that she hasn't fit into for many moons. She hangs them on a hook on the back of her bedroom door, so they will remind her of who she'll be when she loses the weight—light, colourful and vibrant.

Chapter 5

"There are many aspects to your personality—and your weight or dress size is not one of them."

—Joyful Eating

⌒◡

Jenni looks up from her desk as three customer service ladies exit the bathroom. They're pretty hard to miss, given they're giggling and talking loudly to one another. Mora notices her. 'Jenni, we're heading out shopping over lunch,' she calls out across the upstairs office, clearly unable to contain her excitement, 'there's a sale. Would you like to join us?'

'Oh… no. You go ahead without me. I've got a lot of work to do here.' Jenni waves them goodbye.

Yet she doesn't have too much work today. It's just that she can't imagine anything worse than wandering around a clothing store where nothing fits. Her female colleagues would be cackling at one another as they tried on clothing, just like the girls did in high school.

Other women called shopping for clothing 'retail therapy'. Yet Jenni's experiences of clothing shopping felt more traumatising than relaxing or pleasurable.

Sitting at her desk, Jenni recalls her high school friends going to the shops after school to try on clothes for fun. They would laugh at one another if something looked ridiculous and goo and gaa over something that accentuated how beautiful they were. She'd hear their comments; *can you believe this is a size eight? The last dress I tried on was a size twelve.* As if it was an accomplishment.

Jenni has spent many lonely hours outside changing rooms. However, being alone outside the changing rooms was not as mortifying as being inside those four walls.

She hated trying to manoeuvre in the confined space, piling up clothes on a small stool, or having the clothing protrude out of the wall on hooks, reducing the space further. The stools or bench seats, if provided, appeared to be made for kindergarteners, far too small for her oversized arse. She'd have to stand to try on pants, pressing her backside against a wall to steady herself. She absolutely detested having her substantial butt or an elbow rattle the door or push against a curtain, as if calling out to the sales attendants or other women in the changing rooms to say, *Hey! There's a big girl in here.*

More so than the changing rooms, Jenni hated shopping with friends, anyone for that matter. She hated when they'd ask her how an item looked and whether she'd step out of the changing room for them to inspect an article of clothing. If she dared to step out, thinking maybe what she had on would suffice to cover the expanse of her body, she'd often hear comments such as, *I think that colour is far too bright for you, or smaller dots would be more flattering.* Jenni knew the underlying message was a big girl shouldn't wear anything that draws attention. Through many humiliating experiences, she'd learnt that shopping escapades were not for her.

Anyway, with time, as her weight and size increased, most trend stores didn't stock clothing in her size. The message was loud and clear—your body is wrong.

She was relegated to plus-size stores that stocked clothing more suitable for mature women. Or that seemed to be thrown together as an afterthought—oh yes, we nearly forgot that larger ladies exist—rather than being tailored and designed to look good on women in larger bodies. Again, the underlying message was your body is wrong, and you don't deserve to look good.

For these reasons, Jenni mostly wears plain colours. Mainly black stretchy material, in shapeless or loose-fitting styles that camouflage her bulges. It's almost a uniform she deems to be safe: ankle-length skirts and flowy pants, long black tops with ample room around the waist. They are items neither in nor out of fashion and provide no statement of who she is. If she feels particularly inspired, she could add a dash of colour with a scarf or cardigan, but it isn't like she has any style, anyway.

Now Becca, she has style. Why even Norelle has style. Norelle can wear jeans with funky belts, fitted jackets or tunic tops, chunky jewellery and expressive scarves. Jenni resolves that when she loses her excess weight, she'll find her style.

And in some ways, she already has it... hidden behind the hard to cram shut wardrobe. Her wardrobe bulges with clothes that once fit—colourful dresses and skirts, sleeveless shirts and figure forming jackets. She even has knee-high boots from her uni days she can no longer zip up. She keeps all these items, hoping she'll one day fit into them again, but also as a reminder of who she wants to be.

Although she pretty much wears a uniform of black, Jenni has found online shopping a godsend. It enables her to try on clothes without anyone knowing. She can restrict her search results to her size and then try on clothing in privacy. And although it is disheartening to send back items that don't fit, at least no one knows. Online shopping is another reason that baggy, stretchy black articles of clothing have become a staple in her wardrobe; they're more likely to fit and thus mitigate the need to return items so frequently.

Online shopping also enables Jenni to indulge her desire for a smaller body. She can scroll through endless clothing options and fantasise about what she would wear when she loses the weight. Sometimes, in a moment of weakness, she even purchases an item she dreams of wearing one day—something she couldn't do in a store for fear of judgement and questioning.

She knows it is foolish to purchase clothes she doesn't fit into, but they serve a purpose. They hang in her wardrobe and on the bedroom door as motivation and a reminder of who she will be once she loses the weight.

However, every day for over a decade, Jenni has reached into her wardrobe for the safe stretchy selection of black clothes that say nothing of who she is. Because her body is not who she wants to be. She can't show who she is because she doesn't even know the woman she sees in the mirror. She doesn't want to get to know her. She wants the woman in the mirror to vanish so she can be her real self.

As Jenni arranges her desk ready for the following morning, Norelle wanders in flushed for having spent the day out on one of her escapades: a sports event, tree planting, or whatever it is she does.

'Afternoon, Jenni. I've had a big day in the community garden, with kids and dirt everywhere. It was loads of fun.' She smiles and then sighs. 'But phew! I'm exhausted. How are you?'

'You know, can't complain.'

Norelle sits on Pam's chair, who has already left for the day. 'Are you sure everything's okay?'

The sincerity of Norelle's question brings tears to Jenni's eyes. 'Oh, it's completely silly.' She shrugs. 'The... the customer service ladies from downstairs went out shopping at lunch. And I don't know. It just made me feel a little flat.'

'Why do you think it made you feel that way?' Norelle gently enquires.

'Well, I think that's pretty obvious,' Jenni states emphatically, 'how could checking out clothes I could never wear and hearing women half my size state they look fat in something, feel good?'

'Okay. So, you feel flat. What else do you feel?'

'Annoyed... pathetic. Um... Angry.'

'Can you explain in what way you feel angry?'

'I'm angry that they didn't think to invite me until just before leaving the office. I'm angry that there wouldn't even be anything in the store that I could wear, even if I wanted to go. I'm angry with my body!' Jenni can't believe she's allowed herself to get hysterical at work and is relieved most of the staff have already gone home. 'I'm angry that I can't ever be one of the *girls*: I've... I've always been on the outside looking in.' Jenni wipes at the tears beginning to roll down her cheeks.

Norelle hands Jenni a tissue. 'And what is it to be on the inside?'

Jenni hesitates a moment and takes a deep breath to collect her thoughts. 'It is to fit in, to be normal, to be like everyone else. To... to not stand out and feel so damn fucking conspicuous!'

'And then what?'

In defeated frustration, Jenni forces out between sobs, 'I don't know...'

Norelle sits silently, giving Jenni a moment to collect herself. She then continues her gentle questioning. 'What would you have if you fit in with everyone else?'

'Ummm...' Jenni throws the tissue in her wastepaper basket and then sits back, making direct eye contact with Norelle. Norelle does not indicate what she's getting at. She remains perfectly still as she gives Jenni her full attention.

'Ummm... I'd feel content,' Jenni shrugs her shoulders as she continues, 'I'd no longer have this nagging internal voice telling me I'm not good enough.'

'So, what you really want is to feel content?' Norelle confirms.

'I suppose. I've… I've never thought of it like that.'

'Jenni, what if I were to tell you it is not your body you need to change but the thoughts in here?' Norelle says, gently tapping her temple, 'to feel content.'

Jenni is unconvinced. 'I… I don't know. I don't really see how that's possible.'

'Jenni, for your entire life, you've been led to believe the way you look measures your self-worth. That if you just fit in, everything would be fine. However, I'd hazard a guess even if you were the size of those ladies that went out shopping today, that internal voice that tells you you aren't good enough, would remain.' Norelle shrugs. 'Most of us have it. It's pretty normal. The thing that needs to change is not your body. It is the internal dialogue that says you aren't good enough exactly as you are.'

Jenni is silent. Is it her thoughts that affect how she feels, not her body?

'Would you like to head out and talk some more?' Norelle offers.

'No, I think I need to marinate on this a little longer.' Jenni smiles. 'How about a cuppa before work tomorrow?'

'Sounds good. I need an early one tonight, anyway.' Norelle gestures to her dirty knees, evidence of her physically demanding day.

'So, see you downstairs at eight?' Jenni suggests.

'Perfect.' Norelle stands and gives Jenni's shoulder a gentle squeeze before she leaves. 'See you tomorrow, love.'

'Goodnight.'

⁂

On the train ride home, Jenni watches the scenery flash by in a trance. It's as if her mind has emptied and is in a silent void.

Only one question remains: was it her thoughts that made her feel pathetic and worthless, not her body? Did her thoughts hurt her more than her body?

After a microwave meal of honey stir-fry chicken, Jenni wraps her arms around herself as she contemplates how she has inflicted suffering on herself. She falls asleep early, hugging a spare pillow on the couch in a foetal position.

ॐ

The next morning Jenni feels lighter, somehow. She feels a weightlessness of releasing some of her self-deprecating thoughts.

After dressing and applying her make-up, she slices a banana into a bowl and tops it with some yogurt. Examining the bowl, she decides to sprinkle on some sunflower seeds.

She sits, eating in silence, feeling the sunflower seeds resist against her teeth as contrasted by the soft and yielding banana and yoghurt. She notices how she doesn't feel the need for voluminous amounts of food to feel satisfied. She feels she is beginning to notice her body's hunger cues of when, what and how much she needs to eat and how much easier it is when her mind is in a calm and quiet state.

When Jenni arrives at the café early, she orders a tall latté and sits by the window.

'Morning, Jenni,' Norelle sings as she sits down opposite her.

'Morning,' Jenni returns.

'How are you feeling this morning?' Norelle asks.

'Ummm… much better than yesterday,' Jenni assures her, 'but, I'm… I'm not sure I fully comprehend how it is my thoughts that need to change and not my body. But even contemplating that has made me feel calmer, somehow. Yet… I don't know. I'm feeling… I'm feeling a little lost, I suppose.'

'That's totally normal, Jenni. It's normal to feel adrift when you realise it's the voices in your head, not the reality of the situation, that bring you pain and suffering.'

'The reality of the situation?' Jenni gives a questioning look.

'Yes, the reality of the situation is what we perceive through our five senses; our sense of sight, sound, smell, touch and taste.'

'Okay,' Jenni says, comprehending the concept thus far.

'Well, our five senses are the only reality—the only truth. Our minds are what take us out of the reality of what is occurring in the moment. It is our mind that creates interpretations, judgements and explanations of the sensory input. And it is these thoughts, or a resistance to reality, that cause us emotional distress.'

'Okay. But in this moment, I can sense I'm fat,' Jenni challenges.

'Yes, in this moment, you can sense how it feels to be in your body. You can feel your backside on the chair. You can feel clothing against your skin. You may be able to feel your waistband digging into your flesh. However, these are all sensations that are neither good nor bad.'

Norelle maintains her focused gaze as she continues, 'Jenni, it is your mind that tells you that something is wrong with *what is*. It is not your body but your resistance to *what is* that brings you emotional distress. It is your mind that tells you the way your body is right now is wrong.'

'But it is wrong, isn't it?' Jenni partially questions and partially states.

'That is a lie you've been led to believe, Jenni. Your body is perfect as it is in this moment because it is. We've been led to believe that fighting against or resisting *what is*, in this moment, is productive. As if it will stimulate motivation and action. However, if we take action believing we are wrong, we are likely to take unsustainable and potentially destructive actions. It can cause us to take action that is so controlling that when it all gets too hard, we want to rebel and throw in the towel.'

Norelle pauses a moment. 'I believe we need to take action from a place of accepting *what is* in the moment.'

'Do you mean accepting my body as it is right now?' Jenni enquires sceptically.

'Yes,' Norelle confirms.

'But wouldn't that mean I'd just let my body go—I'd allow my weight to balloon out of control?'

'That unfortunately, is another lie you've been led to believe,' Norelle clarifies. 'Accepting your body doesn't mean you won't take care of it. It is about no longer fighting it. It is the fighting and resistance to *what is* that is the problem.'

'Okay... but isn't my body wrong?' Jenni presses.

'In what way?'

'Well, I think that is pretty obvious—I'm fat.' Jenni states insistently.

Norelle nods for Jenni to continue.

'Well... it's clearly unhealthy to be fat.'

'Not necessarily,' Norelle states, 'just as being slim isn't a guarantee of health, nor is being in a larger body a guarantee of being unhealthy.'

'I suppose.'

'The thing is Jenni, we live in a society that perpetuates a fear of fatness. We're led to believe our bodies tell the world something about who we are. If our body is considered overweight, then we must be unhealthy, greedy, lazy, pathetic, worthless. However, these are only stories. They're not reality—they're not the truth.'

'Yep, I've heard these stories many times,' Jenni says with slight resignation.

'Not only are these stories rife in our society, fear of fatness even biases the scientific research that correlates certain disease risks to weight. In research, weight is often used as a proxy for health. However, there is often no consideration of what other factors correspond with weight gain or weight loss.'

Norelle's passion for the topic is evident. 'Researchers often don't, or can't, decipher weight loss from lifestyle behaviours. So, for example, a study that shows an improvement in a health marker with weight loss often ignores the fact that healthy lifestyle behaviours were adopted and could account for a health improvement, irrespective of weight. At any size, people can adopt lifestyle behaviours to improve their health, with or without weight loss.'

'Huh.' Jenni takes a moment to allow Norelle's words to sink in. 'So, you're saying, rather than focusing on weight loss, I should focus on doing things to improve my health?'

'Only if you want to. It's not like you have a moral obligation to be healthy. However, fooling yourself that you are trying to lose weight for health is flawed.'

'Okay... but what if I don't like my body?'

'Jenni, the disliking or liking comes from the perception of how your body should look to meet society's standards. We live in a world that assumes we control our bodies, that we somehow chose it and that how it looks says something of who we are. We see our bodies as something to mould and sculpt, rather than as an incredible biological being capable of so much without our conscious effort—without our control.'

Norelle takes a sip of coffee before continuing, 'Our bodies can take a breath without us being conscious of it. Our bodies pump thousands of litres of blood and replicate billions of cells daily without our knowing. Our bodies enable us to live and experience our lives. Our bodies are not projects to be worked on. They are not something that is broken and needs to be fixed. Rather, they are our vehicle through which we experience life. The belief our bodies are broken or need fixing is a construct of our society and is perpetuated by companies trying to make a buck from our dissatisfaction. In this way, others profit from us hating our bodies.'

'Huh... I'd never... I'd never thought of it like that. But is it possible to want to change our bodies just for ourselves?'

'Jenni, we may take action to feel good, to challenge our bodies and to live our lives in a way that enables us to feel our most vibrant and alive. However, I truly believe any wanting to change our bodies comes from an external desire to make our bodies *right*. However, all this does is generate resistance to *what is* in this moment. It detaches us from the bodies we are in right now. When I believe it is an awareness of *what is* in this moment that enables us to take more self-nurturing and constructive steps.'

'But doesn't that bring us right back to our weight ballooning as we eat as many cupcakes as we want?'

'Jenni, we may believe we eat cupcakes for joy and at times we do. However, the fear of eating excessive quantities or our eating spiralling out of control, well, that is the result of diet culture, not that we can't trust ourselves around food. When we release the notion our weight is a *problem* and diets are the *solution*, we find our relationship to food becomes more intuitive and joyful.'

'So, I need to stop resisting my body and desiring weight loss?'

Norelle confirms with a high pitch, 'Uh-huh.'

'It sort of... sounds wonderful and scary all at the same time,' Jenni says with a contemplative sigh.

Norelle grins. 'It is when you go against the rest of society and live your life for you.'

They sip their coffees in silence, absorbing the caffeine and conversation. Jenni wonders if she should ask Norelle's opinion about weight loss surgery. However, she decides to keep it to herself for now. She feels she already knows what Norelle's response to the question would be and doesn't want to hear it.

Jenni decides to continue the conversation in the direction Norelle is taking it. 'Your way of thinking is so different from how I've thought of my body my entire life. It contradicts so much of what we hear in mainstream and social media. We're told our bodies and health are a choice—that fat is bad and we can control whether or not we're fat,' Jenni says, thinking of how hard she's worked to lose weight in the past—she's been anything but lazy. Yes, she's had plenty of times of excessive eating, but she now considers how that has been the result of restriction and frustration in herself. Just like the surgeon had said, could it be it was never due to a personal weakness? Could it be the problem is diet mentality?

Norelle continues, 'Control is an illusion, Jenni. We don't control the genes we are allotted, the parents we are born to, or our upbringing. We don't control how our body responds to the input we provide it—the environment, food and situations. Control is a lie. A lie that keeps us struggling and fighting *what is*.'

'Hmmm…' Jenni thinks a moment. 'But I've seen health gurus talk about our ability to control whether certain genes are expressed. So, we do have some control, don't we?'

'Yes and no,' Norelle responds, 'yes, we can influence our bodies and the genes that are switched on or off. But no, we don't control it. We can't be absolutely certain a particular action will turn a gene on or off or that a behaviour will ensure health. We can take action to promote health, but we don't control the outcome. People that live what others may consider a healthy lifestyle still confront diseases. And we've all heard stories of a ninety-year-old that smoked their entire life and is in good health. It's the guarantee we need to let go of. As it is thinking this way that causes us to take on an all-or-nothing or must-achieve mentality, which then leads to unsustainable action or yo-yo dieting.'

'I can attest to that, Norelle.' Jenni gestures to her body. 'I've spent my whole life fighting my body and look where that's got me. But… but what about something like weight loss surgery, doesn't that have a guarantee of success?' Jenni asks, finding the perfect time to ask the question without implicitly stating she is considering it.

'I'm no expert, Jenni. But it is my understanding that many of those who have the surgery gain the weight back after a few years. It's not a quick fix or a fix that lasts for life. It's more like a diet you sign up to for the rest of your life.'

'Ohhh... I hadn't... I hadn't realised that.' Jenni looks down at her empty coffee cup.

'And most importantly, it doesn't necessarily deal with the underlying self-deprecating thoughts. Changing your body is not a sure-fire way to quieten the voice in here.' Norelle taps her temple.

'Hmmm...,' Jenni sighs without raising her eyes.

'Unfortunately, there isn't a shortcut to feeling satisfied in the bodies we have,' Norelle says. She then glances at her watch. 'Oh! Is that the time?'

Jenni, now deep in thought, looks up from her cup. 'Oh...,' she says with mild disappointment.

'We can pick up this conversation some other time if you like. Shall we?' Norelle indicates the door that leads to the Union foyer.

'Morning,' Jenni calls out to Pam as she places her handbag under her desk.

'Good morning.' Pam glances at the time displayed on her computer. 'You're a little later than normal.'

'Oh, I just grabbed a cuppa with Norelle before coming up. Thus, I'm cutting it fine.' She bites her lip as she checks if Priya is anywhere around.

'Coast is clear. Priya's got a regional manager's meeting today,' Pam assures her.

'Phew! How are you?'

'Alright. I'm going to have to eat good today. Brian made enough creamy gnocchi to feed an army last night.'

Jenni nearly tells her she doesn't have to eat it all, but realises it might sound judgey. *It's harder than you think to talk people out of their self-deprecating thoughts*, she thinks. 'It's tricky. Most of us have grown up with the message that we have to eat everything on our plate,' Jenni says.

'And you should see Brian's serves—it's a mound,' Pam declares.

Jenni decides to share, 'I've been learning from Norelle to enjoy each mouthful and eat how much I need to satisfy my hunger and feels good in my body. I'd often eat until I was overly stuffed just so I could feel… I don't know… complete.' Jenni shrugs.

'Well, it would be a challenge with Brian, let me tell you,' Pam matter-of-factly states as she turns back to her computer.

Jenni wonders if that is actually true or if it is a story that Pam has made up. *How often do we do this?* Jenni thinks. *How often do we believe the stories we tell ourselves when they may not be true?*

That night, after a simple grilled cheese sandwich, Jenni plops down on the couch with her laptop in hand. Norelle has her thinking, maybe she's only been searching for the reasons why she should have the weight loss surgery and perhaps she should look into complications or arguments not to go ahead with it. She types into the Google search bar: "why you shouldn't have weight loss surgery".

Before her, in the search results, are numerous blogs and articles detailing the complications of weight loss surgery. There are personal stories of why people decided against weight loss surgery or wished they'd never had it.

As she scrolls down the feed, Jenni comes across a site called GirlOnBariatric, which surprises her because although it is a site with advice and support for those who have had bariatric surgery, the site's author has made a recent video stating why she wouldn't recommend it. She shares in the video how she had her surgery twelve years ago. She talks of the complications she and others have had, including the struggles of excess skin and the cost and risks of additional surgeries, often not mentioned when you are first undergoing the procedure.

GirlOnBariatric talks about how much effort is involved to keep the weight off after the surgery and how people find ways to consume excessive calories when their stomach has been substantially reduced. She talks of the increased incidence of alcohol abuse in those who have had the surgery, as tolerance is reduced, and the effects are more immediate and addictive. And the cracker of it all, she talks about how people's stomachs can expand after surgery. She mentions some of the diets she's recently been trying; a calorie counting body freedom diet and the infamous keto.

Jenni can't believe what she is reading. How has she not found this material that shows a very different side to weight loss surgery? Norelle is right. It is not the quick fix she thought it was.

Jenni hadn't liked the thought of having insertions into her abdomen. She hadn't wanted to take time off work. She hadn't relished the prospect of eating a liquid and then purée diet post-surgery. But until now, she'd thought it was all for something: to lose the weight and feel content in her body. She isn't sure what she wants to do anymore. Should she go ahead with this? She's pleased she hasn't gone along with it yet and can still think it through. If she'd signed up to do it already, she's not sure how she'd feel in this moment.

Chapter 6

"It is more likely that it is your inner critic that's holding you back from living your life to the fullest, not your weight."

—Joyful Eating

The following week, Jenni is roped into joining Norelle for a morning of painting the mural on a noise-reducing barrier somewhere on the northside freeway. She meets Norelle at work, and they head to a community centre where they, among a group of adult volunteers and a school group, are given a safety induction by a council worker. It is the usual common sense: don't step over the barricade, don't cross the freeway, don't distract drivers… *Well, I'm sure to draw the attention of drivers*, Jenni thinks as she squirms her way into the extra-large fluorescent orange hi-vis vest.

She pulls the two pieces of fabric across her chest with some effort and pushes down on the Velcro to secure the sides together, which gape between the strips. She feels humiliated looking at the other adults around her, many of whom look more like they are wearing a loose dress as compared to her overstretched vest.

When they arrive at the site, all piling out of the van, a few cars beep and their drivers wave. Jenni can't imagine feeling any more conspicuous—she's a blimp that will not only distract drivers, but be visible from outer space.

All morning, Jenni is conscious of the tightness of the vest around her mid-section and being on display on the side of the freeway. She can't take her mind off the whoosh of traffic and almost flinches each time a car passes. Not for fear of being hit, as they are a good 50 metres from the road barrier, but by what the passers-by must be thinking. *Why did the fat girl in the fluorescent orange vest cross the road?* she half-jokes to herself, pondering the punchline, which falls flat—*to get out of sight.*

Jenni doesn't get into the painting. She feels unsure of her strokes and finds herself comparing her work to those around her. She feels this is more of an activity for the kids and artists, and this thought makes her feel even more out of place here on the roadside.

Jenni feels utter relief when the morning is over, when she is out of her hi-vis vest and on her way back to the office in Norelle's car, despite the physical discomfort of feeling sticky and sweaty from the morning's escapades. They talk cordially about the mural project and some of the students' and artists' talent on the drive. The conversation feels slightly stilted, just as Jenni has felt all morning. Then Jenni blurts out, 'Phew! I feel so sticky, gross, and… fat.'

'It was pretty warm out there,' Norelle agrees, then pauses a moment. 'Fat?' she questions, glancing toward Jenni.

'Yep, fat,' Jenni confirms, wiping a tissue against the flesh at the base of her neck.

'But fat… fat is not a feeling.' Norelle shoots her a look.

'Sheesh, semantics! Ok, I don't feel fat. I *am* fat!' Jenni says with slight exasperation.

'Is it possible that thinking this way about your body affected your mood today—how much you got into the experience?'

'I don't know,' Jenni lies, knowing all too well she hadn't got into the experience as her attention was on the passers-by and the constant comparing her painting to others.

As if reading her mind, Norelle states, 'Often it is the thoughts in our mind that influence how we experience situations, not the actuality of what is occurring in the moment.'

Jenni remains silent as Norelle parks the car a few blocks from the Union building. 'I hope you don't mind. I thought I'd park here as I have a ceramics class in this building after work and thought it would be easier.'

'No worries,' Jenni confirms, although she feels more sweaty thigh rub coming on.

As they walk, Norelle nods towards the city library. 'Do you mind... I have a book on hold to pick up.'

'Not a problem.'

Jenni follows Norelle across the street and up the stairs into the sizeable angular glass building. As Norelle makes her way to the holds counter, she glances toward a row of tables positioned against the glass.

'Oh, I've just seen someone I know,' Norelle says as she makes her way over to a lady sitting with a laptop. She tentatively taps the lady on the shoulder, clearly trying not to startle her.

The lady turns.

When she sees Norelle, she leaps to her feet and hugs her. As they slowly pull away, she looks Norelle directly in the eyes. 'It's so lovely to see you, Norelle.'

'And you.' Norelle turns to Jenni. 'Tansy, this is my friend and colleague, Jenni.'

'Hello, Jenni. Lovely to meet you,' Tansy says, looking to Jenni.

'Hi. Are you working here in the library?' Jenni asks.

'Sort of,' Tansy replies, 'I work part-time and write part-time. I write to help clarify my ideas. I find that being in different environments helps the creative process. Thus, why I'm here in the library.'

'And it's a lovely view.' Norelle indicates the view from the glass windows.

Jenni glances around. She can't imagine spending her spare time here.

'Talking creative endeavours... how's the potting going, Norelle?' Tansy glances at Jenni. 'Norelle is an incredible potter. Have you ever seen her at work? She's so in flow when she's at her wheel.'

'I'm in my potting shed every chance I can get! At the moment, I've been experimenting with different texture finishes,' Norelle says with enthusiasm.

'That's great. I'd love to see what you've been working on,' Tansy gushes.

'You too, Tansy.' Norelle motions to the laptop. 'Let's catch up soon. We've got to get back to work. But it was lovely to see you here in your flow.' They exchange a quick hug before Norelle heads over to the counter to check out her book.

Jenni glances at the book as Norelle scans it, "A New Earth". She's heard of it before, but it seemed too hippie spiritual for her. Norelle notices Jenni's expression. 'I'm reading it on Tansy's recommendation.'

'Oh... what did you both mean before when you said you were "in the flow" with potting and her with writing?'

'Being in a state of flow, or what some people call the zone, is a state of being where you're so absorbed by an activity that you don't think of anything else. It takes you away from your thoughts and brings you into the present moment.'

'Makes sense.'

As they head back to the office, Norelle asks, 'What do you do where you feel in a state of flow?'

'Um... I don't know. I like to read. But nowadays, I mostly just watch TV when I get home. I don't feel I have the time or energy for hobbies—I mean, *flow activities*.' Jenni gives a cheeky grin.

'What about cooking? Does that bring you into a state of flow?' Norelle suggests.

'I don't think so. I don't really enjoy it. Or do it that often. I'm more of a microwave it... or frozen veggies alongside chicken kind of person.'

'What do you do just for the fun of it, which takes you away from your worries?' Norelle asks.

'So apart from reading and watching TV?'

'Yes. They aren't what we'd consider flow activities, as they don't require your full attention. Flow activities are things like playing a musical instrument, mountain biking, learning a language... that sort of thing.'

'Nope, I don't do anything like that,' Jenni declares.

'Maybe not now. But when you were younger, was there anything that you'd do that would absorb your attention for hours at a time?'

'Uhm...' Jenni wracks her brain. 'Oh, I used to scrapbook and arrange flowers as a child. My mother loved to garden, and I'd collect flowers and arrange them for her. I used to experiment with pressing them and sticking them in my scrapbooks. I'd combine them with coloured papers, ribbons and images I'd cut out of mum's gardening magazines. I loved exploring the contrast of colours and textures.'

'And why did you stop?'

'I... I don't know. I guess I got busy with study. Then work,' Jenni says. 'I never got back into it. There didn't really seem to be any point.'

'That is the point, Jenni. It's not about whether what you create is worth something to anyone. It's about the process. It's about taking the time in that state. When was the last time you scrapbooked or arranged flowers?'

Jenni shrugs. 'Oh, I don't know... a few decades.'

'Would you like to do it again?'

'I suppose.' She shrugs again. 'But I don't have the time and it's sort of a waste of money.' Jenni wrinkles up her nose. 'It just doesn't seem worth it.'

'Except for the joy it brings you and the beauty it brings into your life,' Norelle states pointedly. 'Do you think it is worth time and money for joy and beauty?'

'I hadn't thought of it like that,' Jenni marvels.

'And you... do you think that you are worth it?'

'Um... what do you mean?'

'Do you feel you deserve joy and beauty in your life?'

Whoa, Jenni thinks, *do I deserve joy and beauty, to spend time and money just for the fun of it and to get into the flow?*

Jenni spends money on fun activities: movies, meals out, bottles of wine. She doesn't deprive herself of joy. Or does she?

As she thinks about it, she realises the activities she partakes in are more socially acceptable. Yet arranging flowers or scrapbooking they are somehow intimate—it's just for her.

Jenni is grateful they've now reached the office building, so she doesn't have to answer Norelle's question. 'Better get back to it. I feel I've got a lot to process after our walk.' She smiles. 'Thanks, Norelle.'

⌀

'Finally, the contract has gone through.' Becca is leaning over Amanda's desk with a grin on her face.

'Oh, that's so exciting. What are you thinking of doing to celebrate?' Amanda whispers in an excited tone, as if she's in on a secret.

'We're thinking of having a beach party. I'll let you know what we decide.'

The gorgeous couple, Becca and Adam, have purchased a beach apartment on the Sunshine Coast. Somewhere that Becca could show off her spray tan and perfect body and drink Mojitos or some other elegant low-cal drink by the beach. Jenni can't imagine anything worse.

Jenni remembers loving swimming but has rarely swum in a pool or the ocean since she was a child. She did own a swimsuit, though she seldom wore it. If she did, she kept it covered under a kaftan or some other flowy beach dress; never to see the light of day or be immersed in water.

She was seven when she became conscious of her body size at the beach after her father had made that offhand comment about her needing to watch her weight. From then on, she'd felt too conspicuous in a swimsuit. And by her teens, she'd stopped swimming altogether.

Jenni missed splashing in the waves and the sense of freedom of being immersed in water, but her refusal to swim wasn't much of an issue. She'd always found an excuse not to go in the water, apart from the one time when Paul had a conference in tropical Port Douglas.

Jenni remembers it vividly. Paul couldn't understand why she wouldn't want to go on a holiday where his company covered the room cost, and she could spend her day soaking up the sunshine and relaxing by the pool. That was exactly why she didn't want to go. She didn't want to spend her days lying around a pool with people she hardly knew, making small talk in the evenings, all the while exposing her body. She couldn't see how it would be enjoyable. To her, it was a nightmare.

Her refusal to go had led to an argument. Paul couldn't see what the problem was. He wanted to fit in with his buddies at the conference, who were all bringing their partners. 'Who in their right mind would forgo an expense-paid mid-winter tropical holiday?' he'd asked.

However, Jenni wouldn't budge. She couldn't possibly put on a swimsuit and frolic around in the pool while Paul attended the conference. She had spent her entire life avoiding these types of situations. Her fear of being judged intensified her response to Paul and soon escalated the argument. She knew she was being irrational and unreasonable, but she was upset he couldn't see her point of view.

She remembers that night when Paul went to bed, she had snuck into the kitchen to devour the remaining ice cream, which was a common occurrence when they disagreed on something. It was her opportunity to rebel.

Jenni then overhears Becca and Amanda scheming about a joint housewarming and kids' birthday party at the beach. The thought of time at the beach with colleagues fills her with horror. She is relieved they are excluding her from the conversation.

The next day, Norelle spends most of the day in one of the glass meeting rooms interviewing and phoning entertainers for a festival the Union is sponsoring in collaboration with the council and arts centre to inspire creativity.

Mid-afternoon, when Jenni pours herself a cuppa, she pops her head into the meeting room. 'How's it going, Norelle?'

'Phew! It's a lot to plan—logistics, logistics.' Norelle smiles. 'I'm not used to spending all day in the office—how do you do it?'

'I suppose I could say the same to you regarding coordinating kids and community activities,' Jenni comments.

Norelle shoots her a smile. 'Each to their own, I suppose.'

Jenni nods, as Norelle comments, 'Well, I'm looking forward to getting out of here.' Then glancing at her watch, she continues, 'One of the performers I met this morning told me they are performing in the Botanic Gardens this evening. What do you say—would you like to join me for a puppeteering musical comedy?'

'Oh!' Jenni says in surprise. *When was the last time anyone invited me to go out somewhere in the city?* 'What time?' Jenni asks as it's only gone three.

'Oh, I think it's around 5.30 pm. So, we could walk down together straight after work.'

'Sure thing! I'm up for it.' Jenni grins.

'It will be great to get some fresh air,' Norelle puffs. 'Oh, and let Pam know she's welcome to join us. I've just got another five calls to make and a few emails, and then hopefully, I'm done,' Norelle sighs as she looks to the table, strewn with papers and pamphlets.

'See you later, then,' Jenni chirps as she leaves Norelle to it.

She returns to her desk with a skip to her step. She mentions going out to Pam, but she says something about Brian expecting her to make the evening meal tonight. *Oh, the benefits of being single*, Jenni muses.

As Jenni and Norelle walk to the Botanic Gardens, Norelle tells Jenni about the various performers she'd spoken to during the day—magicians, musicians, contortionists, comedians, poets, clowns and face painters. She laughs as she describes some of the performers and their talents. 'It's incredible what people dedicate their time to perfect. I can't imagine how some of them come up with their ideas. Their creativity and imagination are amazing and somewhat infectious,' she says with a smile and more bounce in her step, now she is away from the office.

The show is corny but hilarious, and Jenni finds herself laughing out loud along with the children and adults in the audience spread out across the grass beneath the dappled shade. After the show, Norelle and Jenni take a walk, and when they come across a wine bar overlooking the river, Norelle suggests they have a drink. It has been a long time since Jenni has simply allowed herself to enjoy an evening without feeling conspicuous or self-conscious. Norelle orders them a small platter, and they pick at it as they talk, enjoying the food, wine and atmosphere.

Norelle tells Jenni how she had divorced when her children left home and had felt lost with what she wanted to do with her life. She explains how much of her life had been about caring for them, and when they left home and her husband moved out, she had to rediscover who she was and what she wanted from life. It was at this time she began to read more and trained as a community worker.

Jenni is enjoying Norelle's company and orders a second drink.

Sometime later, Norelle, only having had one drink, offers to drive Jenni home. Jenni accepts, feeling a sense of familiarity with Norelle she never expected when she first met her. She never imagined she'd find a friend in this curious and non-conforming woman.

Watching the lights through the car window, as they make their way out of the city, Jenni starts, 'Thanks for a wonderful evening, Norelle. I haven't done anything like this in a while. I sometimes forget how lovely the city is. I often only think of it as a place to work and forget it is a place to relax and play. I'll have to make a point of getting out and exploring the city more often.'

Norelle nods. 'Yes, there is so much to see and do. And the river and Botanic Gardens are simply wonderful places to just... *be*.'

'They sure are. And tonight, I felt that... a sense of just being. I felt so... uninhibited. I don't know... somehow, I felt like I was no longer in this body?' Jenni looks down to the rolls around her waist above the seat belt. Somehow, as the alcohol's effect fades, she feels the disgust and resentment toward her body return.

'Jenni, it is likely you felt that way because you were no longer occupied by the thoughts in your mind, but were feeling into your body. It is possible the alcohol helped to quieten the internal dialogue.'

Jenni contemplates this for a moment. 'Or did I simply forget that I am in this body?'

'Or you need to stop thinking about your body being wrong entirely?' Norelle suggests as she turns onto Jenni's street.

'I don't know... I want to feel uninhibited and free—I have to gain control of my weight to do that.'

'Jenni, you can feel uninhibited and free in the body you have right now. It's about changing your thinking, not your body.'

'I don't know.'

Norelle pulls up at Jenni's house, turns off the engine and faces her. 'Jenni, tell me this: do you believe there is a thin girl inside you, waiting to be set free?'

'Well... sort of.' Jenni winces.

'And this thin girl who lives inside you, who is she?'

'Well, she's not a separate person to me. She is me, or at least who I'll be when I lose the weight.'

'And what will *she* be able to do that you can't?'

Jenni considers this a moment and then the thoughts flow out of her... '*she'll* be able to walk down the street without people taking a second glance or saying something insulting. *She'll* be able to eat her lunch without everyone inspecting what she's eating. *She'll* be able to go to work and not be viewed as lazy or less ambitious than others. *She'll* be able to ride a bicycle or dive into a pool without people thinking *good on her.*'

Jenni takes a deep breath, feeling a sense of release.

'And what else will *she* be able to do that you can't?' Norelle inquires further.

'Everything!' Jenni exclaims, suddenly feeling sober. '*She* won't feel so alone. *She'll* travel. *She'll* be able to go anywhere. *She* won't avoid parties, clubs, bars, beaches, amusement parks, aeroplanes or going to cafés alone. *She* won't feel embarrassed and ashamed to be seen or take up space in the world.'

Jenni takes a moment to collect her thoughts. 'I… I can't see any way around it, Norelle. I have to lose this weight.' Sighing, she continues. 'I get where you're coming from with the conscious eating and accepting your body stuff, but I need to lose this weight and fast. If I get to forty and I am still here.' She glances down at her body. 'I don't know.' She wraps an arm around her chest and holds her head in the other, feeling she is teetering on the verge of tears.

Norelle gives Jenni a sympathetic look. 'I understand.'

'No… no, you don't understand, Norelle. You don't know what it is like to be my size. You don't know what it's like to have others look at you. You don't know what it's like to wear your shame every single day for everybody to see. You don't know what it's like to stand out when all you want is to fit in. I can't hide it. It is not like self-harming or being an alcoholic, where I can hide my shame behind closed doors. I am exposed for everyone to see my weakness.'

Norelle listens attentively. 'You're right. I don't know what it is like to be you,' Norelle says sympathetically.

'Fuck! I don't want your sympathy, Norelle! I don't need it. I don't want to be someone others resent or feel sympathy for.' She takes a deep breath. 'I want to be confident. I want to be bold. Flamboyant and loud. I want to be unapologetically me.' She glances at Norelle. 'You don't get it—I can't be that in this body.' Jenni jerks her hands to indicate her waist. 'This… this is not what I want, Norelle.'

Norelle is silent a moment, then speaks softly, 'I want you to consider something, Jenni.' Jenni turns to face her. 'What if it's not possible for you to ever be thin? What if there is no *one day*? What if this is your real life right now? What if you're already living it?'

'I'm not.' Jenni refuses to budge her thinking.

'But what if you are—what if this is your real life?' Norelle asks tenderly.

'Then... then, I don't see the point.' As soon as the words escape her mouth, Jenni wishes she hadn't said them. She doesn't really mean it. She wants to live, just not in this body. 'You... you know I didn't mean that,' she clarifies, trying to make light of her comment.

Norelle is silent a moment and then gently says, 'I understand, but is it possible you've made enjoying your life conditional on your weight—when you have so much life in you right now?'

'I just don't know how... how to love this body?' Jenni glances downwards, holding back tears.

'You don't necessarily have to love it, Jenni. Just stop fighting it. Stop punishing yourself for it. Stop withholding joy and happiness until it changes. Enjoy what you have—a body that enables you to live life.'

Jenni manages a small smile. 'I'll try,' she whimpers, opening the car door. 'I'll try,' she says again as she closes it behind her.

She notices Norelle's car doesn't move as she makes her way into her apartment. But she doesn't look back.

In her silent kitchen, Jenni makes herself a hot chocolate and pushes three marshmallows beneath the surface, watching them bob back up. She takes the mug into her equally quiet loungeroom and takes a seat. She sits on her couch in the near darkness, only illuminated by the kitchen light. She curls her hands around the outside of the mug, feeling the warmth and smelling the bittersweet aroma.

In the quietness, with tears in her eyes, she acknowledges she reaches for food to feel—she can admit it now—love. The tears escape her eyelids and begin to run down her cheeks. She wipes them away with her free wrist while her focus does not wander away from the only love she knows—food.

Then an overwhelming feeling of disgust washes over her. She feels disgust not only for her body but towards the hot chocolate. How had she allowed food to have so much control over her life? *Who the fuck is in charge here*? she angrily wonders.

Jenni gets up off the couch and makes her way back to the kitchen, dumping the untouched hot chocolate into the sink. She washes away the milky brown liquid and then squashes the marshmallows under the running hot water, so they melt and disappear down the drain hole.

She turns off the tap and heads straight to bed so she can wake refreshed and ready to take back control of her life. Tomorrow she will schedule the follow-up consultation with the surgeon— she's got no choice but to go ahead with it.

Chapter 7

"... maximise your feeling of vitality, happiness and contentment, where your happiness is not dependent on the number on the scales or what you ate the day before."

— Joyful Eating

⁓

'Good morning, Sunshine Weight Loss Solutions. You're speaking with Deb. How can I bring sunshine into your day?'

Jenni sits on the other end of the phone, motionless. She… she can't do it—an IV drip, sedatives, incisions, staples, sutures…

Deb's chirpy voice cuts into the silence. 'Hello?'

I can't. I can't do this to my body. But, I… I can't be fat. But, I… I can't have surgery. Jenni deliberates in silence and then hears the beeps that indicate that Deb has given up on her. Like she has so many times before, given up on herself.

⁓

That day at work, Jenni purposefully ignores Norelle and avoids personal conversation with Pam. She feels like she's on the verge of a breakdown and simply wants to pull herself through the day.

She is grateful she made the phone call before anyone else arrived at work, as she isn't sure how she'd have explained the stupor she found herself in. After the call, she'd sat there numb, motionless, for she has no idea how long.

She has no idea what she'll do next. Only when she hears the suction of the door downstairs opening does she pour herself a tea and get to work.

Jenni works all day on autopilot. She's running through the motions, but she isn't really there. She is nowhere.

When Jenni reaches her apartment, she nearly trips on a package on her doormat. Knowing what it is, she throws it on the hall table and heads to the fridge. She feels uninspired and doesn't care what she eats.

She places two slices of bread on a plate and smears them with peanut butter. Then she puts on the TV to cut through the silence and eats the sandwich standing in the kitchen, wondering what she'll do with her evening. She heads to the bedroom to change into a shapeless cotton nightie, preparing for a comfy evening on the couch.

Back in the kitchen, she takes a packet of Monte Carlo biscuits out of the pantry. She sits on the couch and munches away, mesmerised by the TV. She's not watching anything she particularly enjoys. It's some game show, but it allows her to forget about her day. She has to forget that she can't bring herself to go ahead with the surgery.

As she dusts biscuit crumbs from her nightie, she feels like she needs something savoury. She heads to the kitchen for some slices of cheese and salami.

Sitting on the couch, she feels her stomach gurgle with the combination of food. She feels both bloated and deflated. *Who was I kidding that I could ever lose weight,* she thinks. *It is never going to happen.*

Determinedly, she makes her way back to the hall table. Then she heads to the kitchen with the package and retrieves a bottle of Moscato from the fridge. She unscrews the cap and takes a sip straight from the bottle. She takes gulps while twirling the light package on the counter.

Decisively, Jenni takes a pair of scissors from the kitchen drawer and heads to the bedroom. She places the Moscato on her bedside table and then pierces the package with the scissors so she can rip through the plastic, revealing a vibrant azure blue. She pulls the soft material from the package and allows the bag to fall to the floor.

She holds the dress up to her body in front of the wardrobe mirror to imagine what it would look like on her body: how it highlights her blue eyes and brightens her hair. She'd thought she'd feel more confident when she could fit into this knee-length, summery dress. However, right now, feeling bloated and pathetic, she knows this will never happen. She feels tears well up in her eyes as she gazes at the woman in the mirror, so far from who she dreamt of being. That girl is lost forever, and Jenni knows it.

Jenni takes the scissors and stabs them into the fabric. She inserts her fingers into the cut and pulls her hands apart to tear at the material. She feels a warm tear roll down her cheek as she drops the dress to the floor, discarding it like her dreams.

She then turns to the dresses hanging on the back of the bedroom door, reminders of her weight loss goals. She lifts the hem of one dress and cuts as if trying to create a frilled lower half of the dress. She cuts short vertical cuts into the soft, delicate fabric, feeling the material between her fingers. She then takes the shreds of fabric and tears up the length of the dress to the waistband. She tugs at the dress, freeing it off the coat hanger, and continues to rip into it.

As tears streak down her face, Jenni continues to shred at the dresses until she is standing amongst a pile of ripped tatters scattered across her bedroom floor. She feels a sense of relief from her rage. Although she has destroyed the dresses, she still feels defeated because she's not free of the enemy; she is still inside her body.

Overwhelmed with despair, Jenni collapses back onto the bed.

However, in what she thought would be a moment of release, she immediately feels a searing pain in her thigh. 'What the fuck?' she cries out.

'Oh, fuck,' she repeats, seeing she has stabbed herself in the thigh with the scissors.

She rolls to her side and twists her upper body to see where the scissors have penetrated her thigh. She can see the handle of the scissors, but she can't see where they enter her thigh. She feels along her leg for the entrance to the wound, yet she can't tell how deep they've pierced her.

She lifts herself off the bed with her backside up in the air. She backs herself towards the wardrobe mirror so she can see the damage.

'Oh, fuck,' she mutters.

Of course, she sees the scissors protruding from her upper thigh, but what overwhelms her is her arse—the cottage cheese texture of the mass of flesh—and the folds of skin at her waist. The pain of her wound barely registers as the distress of seeing her body in this way overwhelms her.

Her crying becomes hysterical. She has to get medical attention, but she can't face anyone seeing her this way: what will people think she's been doing?

She tries to reach for the scissors and feels a searing pain up her leg as she grazes them with her fingers. Overwhelmed with nausea, she drops forward, bracing herself with her hands, one reaching the bed to soften the fall to her knees. She crawls to her phone on the bedside table.

Should she call 000? *Is it an emergency—fat girl stabs herself?* She can't believe it. She has no other choice. She dials.

'Police, fire and rescue or ambulance?' *All and none of them,* Jenni thinks to herself before responding.

❧

Three stitches later, Jenni is on her way home in an Uber. She is utterly humiliated by the whole palaver... of being rolled into hospital... of the questions about what she'd done... of the nurses and doctors fussing over her.

She isn't used to that much attention. It makes her feel exceedingly uncomfortable. It is why she couldn't bring herself to have weight loss surgery in the end.

No one in the hospital mentioned her weight, but she could hear their thoughts. She'd heard it all before: *if she hadn't been that fat, she'd probably have missed the scissors. If it hadn't been for all that excess padding, the scissors could have hit a bone.*

After the ordeal, Jenni doesn't want to see another soul ever again. Yet, she can't wait until she is a *healthy weight* to face the world. She has to fix it right now... and she knows she needs help to do so. She reaches into her handbag for her mobile phone. 'Norelle... would it be possible to catch up for a cuppa tomorrow at my place?'

When Jenni arrives home, she goes straight to bed, stepping over the shreds of material strewn across the floor. She is tired and fed-up—she no longer cares.

❧

At around 10 am the next morning, there is a knock at the door. Jenni is lying in bed in that state between awake and asleep, still unsure if she really wants to wake up at all. She hobbles to the door in her dressing gown to let Norelle in.

Norelle takes in the dishevelled woman before her. 'Oh dear, what happened?'

'I had a little accident last night,' Jenni says as she slowly walks Norelle into the living room.

'What happened, honey?'

'Norelle, I can't do it anymore. I tried. I've tried so many times to lose this unsightly excess weight,' Jenni stammers, bursting into tears and grimacing as she sits sideways on the couch.

Norelle's look of concern deepens. 'Have you... hurt yourself, Jenni?'

'It was an accident,' Jenni begins, 'I sat on a pair of scissors. The scissors I'd used to destroy my *skinny* clothes.' She nods towards the half-open door. At a glance, Norelle can see the shredded material strewn across the floor.

Norelle takes a moment to process the situation. Then she makes her way to sit beside Jenni. 'I'm so sorry, Jenni,' she says, placing her hand on Jenni's slightly quivering shoulder. They sit there together in silence, aware of one another's presence.

'I... I know that diets don't work, Norelle. But I don't know what the alternative is...' She releases a sob. 'I hate my body... I hate myself....' She turns slightly toward Norelle and feels a pull at her stitches. Wincing, she lets out another sob. 'I don't know what to do, Norelle.'

Norelle sits a moment, taking in Jenni's words. 'Oh... honey, you won't find the answers out there...' She motions to the front door. Then nodding towards the bedroom door. 'Nor will you find answers in beautiful clothing,' she continues, giving Jenni's shoulder a gentle squeeze. 'You have to go within.'

'Um... oh... okay,' Jenni stammers.

'Let's begin... begin with a clean slate,' Norelle starts, looking around the room. 'Let's clear out everything in here that reminds you that you aren't who you want to be.'

Norelle makes her way to Jenni's bedroom and peers in. 'Have you got garbage bags?'

Jenni points toward the door behind her that leads into the kitchen. Once Norelle finds the garbage bags, she heads back to the bedroom.

Jenni lifts herself off the couch cautiously and makes her way to the bedroom door. She watches as Norelle gathers up the shreds of material and stuffs them into a garbage bag. Norelle then motions to the wardrobe. 'Jenni, are there more clothes in there that don't fit you?'

'Many,' Jenni responds.

'Oh, we're going to have to get rid of them. We're going to have to get rid of every reminder in this apartment that you are not the size you want to be right now.' Jenni is not about to argue, although she's not convinced she wants to be the size she is right now.

'I'll start a bag for the charity shop. Take a seat, Jenni.' Norelle motions to the bed.

Jenni watches as Norelle slides open the wardrobe and pulls out one hanger at a time. 'Does this fit you? Does this fit you? Do you enjoy wearing this? Do you feel good in this?'

As the charity bag expands, Jenni's wardrobe becomes sparser. However, rather than feeling nostalgic towards the clothes she's losing, Jenni feels a sense of relief. Although she doesn't feel up to participating in this cull, her shoulders relax as she feels she's shedding the weight she's been holding on to.

When Norelle finishes, she stands, hands-on-hips, inspecting the now spartan wardrobe. 'You might need to get yourself a few more clothes.' She smiles. 'But for now, you can use some of these colourful scarves to change things up a bit.' She nods to herself, clearly satisfied with her work.

A smile begins to spread across Jenni's face. 'Thanks, Norelle. I'm not sure I could have done that alone. But it does feel great.'

'Oh, we haven't finished yet.' Norelle smirks.

'No?'

'No, we have the rest of the apartment to go,' Norelle says as she walks out of the bedroom.

'What do you mean?' Jenni calls out.

Standing in the doorway, Norelle explains, 'We have all those pills and potions, diet books, diet foods, shakes, cellulite scrubs and women's magazines to get out of here. I don't want there to be any more reminders that you are not the weight you want to be.'

'Oh... okay.' Jenni isn't sure if she is overwhelmed or excited as she slides off the bed and limps to where Norelle now is in the bathroom.

'First things first, Jenni,' Norelle says, shooting her a knowing grin, 'we've got to destroy these.' She bends down and takes hold of Jenni's bathroom scales.

Jenni stands silently, bewildered. She has depended on those scales for over twenty years to indicate her weight loss progress. Although, more often than not, the number displayed has not been inspiring but utterly disheartening.

Norelle notices Jenni's hesitation. 'Tell me Jenni, when you hop on these scales and you've lost some weight, how does that make you feel?'

'Good... like I'm making progress.'

'And when you hop on the scales and your weight has increased?'

'Crap. I feel like an utter failure.'

Norelle continues her line of questioning. 'And, how does that make you feel for the remainder of the day?'

'Like I'm a worthless fat lard.' Jenni shrugs.

Norelle motions to the scales. 'Do you want these dictating how you feel every day?'

'No,' Jenni responds warily.

'I say, let's get rid of them. Let's see what life is like without them. Are you prepared to give that a go?'

'Well, they haven't done anything for me so far. So... I suppose... why not? Let's ditch them,' Jenni agrees, a grin appearing on her face.

'Let's not ditch them... let's... let's destroy them,' Norelle says excitedly. 'Have you got a hammer?'

'Yep. In the toolbox under the kitchen sink.'

'Great.' Norelle shows no sign of hesitation as she heads to the kitchen.

Jenni stays standing at the bathroom door as Norelle retrieves the hammer.

'Let's step outside,' Norelle says, opening the balcony door. She places the scales on the concrete and turns to Jenni, offering her the hammer. 'Tell them how you really feel.'

Jenni takes hold of the hammer and looks at the scales. She has believed they would keep her motivated and on track. Yet they haven't done that for her. She hasn't lost weight. Since she first stepped on a set of scales, all her weight has ever done is slowly increased, bit-by-bit, diet-by-diet, weigh-in after weigh-in. She's allowed the scales to dictate her mood. At times, standing on those scales could be an elating experience. Yet more often than not, they would deflate her mood, causing her to struggle through her day, eating meagre portions to satisfy the scales the following day. What value had they added to her life? None.

Jenni feels a wave of exhilaration flow through her body. She raises the hammer over her head, and as she bends her knees, she allows the hammer to smash into the scales.

Only a small dent appears in the centre of the scales. Feeling anger surge through her, Jenni raises the hammer again, and this time she slams it into them. They buckle under the force. The back and front come apart at the edges. She hammers again and again until the two sides are completely separated and the numbers indistinguishable.

As Jenni stands, taking in the remains of the scales at her feet, she feels her heart pounding in her chest. She feels energy coursing through her veins. She barely notices the stitches in her thigh.

'So, how did that feel?' Norelle asks from the corner of the balcony.

'U-n-fucking-b-e-l-i-e-v-a-b-l-e!' Jenni whoops.

'Are you ready to live in a way where your mood is not dictated by the weight on the scales or your dress size?'

'For sure.' Jenni smiles.

'How about you take a shower while I finish up? Then, shall we go out for a late breakfast-early lunch?'

'Sounds good to me,' Jenni jubilantly says, as if she could take on the world.

In the shower, Jenni feels as if she's washing away her old self—the self that didn't think her body measured up. She feels the flesh of her arms and the water falling on her shoulders. She feels a sense that nothing matters, that everything she had previously thought was important isn't important at all. She lives in this body. She is here right now beneath this skin.

After she showers, Jenni takes a seat on the couch, looking at the three garbage bags by the front door. She can't believe she had that many useless reminders that her body wasn't good enough.

⁂

Norelle drives them to an outdoor café in New Farm that serves all-day breakfast. 'I thought you might be in need of a real hearty breakfast today. What do you say?'

'Amen.' Jenni smirks.

While they wait on their English breakfasts, Jenni comments, 'Norelle, seeing those garbage bags on the floor made me think of all the weight I've been holding onto. Not in my body, but mentally. You know?'

Smiling, Norelle simply nods.

'I've realised I've been holding myself back until I lost the physical weight, but I never realised the weight I had to lose was in here.' Jenni gestures to her head.

'Um-hum.'

Jenni laughs. 'You knew that already?'

Norelle shrugs. 'Well, yes and no. I could see how much you held yourself back, that you didn't believe you were good enough... that something needed to change. I could see how you made your happiness conditional on your body and your ability to lose weight, rather than experiencing joy right now, in the body you have.'

Jenni thinks on it a moment. 'That's what I've been doing, isn't it?'

Norelle nods in agreement.

'Well, from now on, my happiness is not going to be conditional on anything. I am going to experience my life as it is right now,' Jenni declares.

Then as the waitress places the two plates before them, Jenni continues, 'Starting right now, I'm going to enjoy every mouthful... every moment... I'm not waiting any longer.' She picks up her knife and fork and slices into her bacon with relish.

Chapter 8

"At any weight or size, you can eat, move and live in ways that nourish your body, with or without weight loss."

— Joyful Eating

Jenni runs a bath. She drops in an essential oil mix, which has been untouched since she put it there last year. It was a secret Santa gift from work.

She tests the water temperature and feels the water drag between her fingers. She lets them linger a moment. Standing, she unties her robe and hangs it on the hook behind the bathroom door.

Completely naked, she gently steps a foot into the bathtub; the heat only just bearable. She then steps her other foot in and braces herself on the sides of the bathtub as she lowers her body into the sweet-scented water. She feels the warm embrace of the water surrounding her thighs, buttocks and stomach as she sits in the tub.

Once the water begins to still, Jenni slides her hands down the sides of the bathtub and onto her thighs. She feels the curve of her hips and the dimpling of her thighs. Then she flexes her toes and notices the upward pressure of contracted muscle under her hands and the definition in her calves.

Still sitting up, she looks at her legs—they have supported her throughout her life. She bends forward and feels down the length of her legs, all the way to her toes. She feels each toe between her fingers and then massages the tops and soles of both feet.

Then she slowly slides her hands up the length of her legs to the crease at her hip flexor. She gently presses her fingers into the roll of flesh where her thighs and stomach meet and feels for her hip bones.

She releases the pressure, allowing her fingers to glide over the outline of her stomach. And with her palms gently laid on her stomach, she feels its roundness. Then, she draws her hands towards her breasts, feeling their soft tenderness. She cups her breasts a moment and then draws her hands across her chest, stroking her shoulders and then skimming down the length of her arms.

She moves her hands over her body with a gentle and curious touch, as if observing it for the first time. *I'm sorry I've neglected you*; she thinks as she lies back, allowing the water to caress her entire body.

Lying in the bathtub, she notices for the first time in her life how good it feels to be in her skin, in her body. She closes her eyes and feels the sensation of water around her. She feels the warmth of her skin and the rhythm of her heartbeat.

She then moves her right hand to the crease where her thighs meet, noticing the roughness of skin where her legs chafe when she wears skirts. She bends her knees and with her fingers, traces the line where her legs meet. Slowly, she parts her legs and strokes her inner thighs tenderly. As she caresses her inner thighs, her index finger ever so slightly grazes between her legs, and she feels an aliveness in her. She sinks into the blissful joy of being in her body. She realises the beauty of her body is in the sensations it can experience and the life it enables her to live, not how it looks. She feels joy in the aliveness beneath her skin.

On Monday morning, Jenni awakes with a sense of peace she hasn't felt for… well… as long as she can remember.

She dresses for work, choosing a colourful scarf that matches her royal blue ballet flats. She then puts on her makeup in an almost meditative way. She doesn't feel rushed nor notice thoughts in her mind. It's as if she is witnessing and feeling into her actions. She tunes into her body and doesn't feel particularly hungry. So, she grabs an apple before leaving the apartment.

Walking along the footpath to the train station, she notices the sunshine on her shoulders, kissing her face and arms. She notices her rhythmic footsteps on the pavement.

She catches the train on time and during the entire trip to work, she feels like she is seeing things for the first time. She has no desire to pull out her phone to pass the time. Instead, she takes in all the colours and shapes, noticing all the things she normally passes without attention.

When she arrives outside the Union building, she purchases a smoothie at the downstairs café. On autopilot, she takes it into the office. But instead of going to her desk to drink it, she sits in the lunchroom. She takes off the lid and observes the incandescent red. Then she sucks up through the straw, feeling the coolness of the liquid on her lips and tongue. She swirls it around in her mouth, observing the flavour and allowing the liquid to warm before she swallows.

She takes another sip with the same awareness, not only of the smoothie but the quietness of the office. It is almost as if she can feel the quiet stillness in her body and the suction of air whenever the door downstairs opens and someone enters. She continues to drink, rhythmically sucking, swallowing and taking a moment to feel into her body between sips.

She's so focused on her smoothie she doesn't notice Barry at the lunchroom doorway. 'Good morning, Jenni,' he says, 'you look... radiant today.'

'Thanks, Barry. It sure is a lovely day,' she responds, realising she's just accepted a compliment without brushing it off.

'Is there any particular reason for your radiance today?' he inquires.

'I... I may have discovered what unconditional love is,' she says, more to herself than to Barry—he'd caught her in a *moment. I can't believe I just said that aloud,* she thinks.

'Oh,' Barry says disappointedly.

Noticing this, Jenni continues, 'Everyone can achieve it, as everyone is worthy of love. I'm only just starting to see that.'

'I'm pleased for you.' Barry nods as he leaves the lunchroom.

Finishing her smoothie, Jenni drops her handbag by her desk and heads to the bathroom to freshen up before she gets to work. Becca is there in her training clothes. She's standing by the basins, untying her shoelaces.

'G-o-o-d morning,' Jenni sings out cheerfully.

'Hi,' Becca replies, looking up as she pushes off her running shoe with her other foot. 'I've had a tough training run today. In two days, I'll be tapering off for the half-marathon in two weeks.' She seems pleased with herself.

'It's incredible what the human body is capable of,' Jenni muses as she washes her hands and checks her teeth for smoothie remnants.

'Sure is... to see how far you can push it,' Becca affirms.

Jenni reflects on Becca's comment a moment before replying, '... and when you feel into it and contemplate what it is capable of without your conscious effort.'

Becca raises her eyebrows, looking slightly confused.

'We're just lucky to be alive in our bodies,' Jenni says, smiling as she exits the bathroom.

The remainder of Jenni's workday flows smoothly. It isn't that the work is any different or easier, but her approach is more relaxed. She does each task with her full attention and gets up and moves her body when she feels she needs to.

When Jenni finishes work, she decides to take a walk while the sun is still shining. She finds herself wandering through the Botanic Gardens, observing the colours and shapes around her. She feels a lightness to her step and a freedom in being in her body.

On her way back to the train station, Jenni contemplates how she might mark this moment—to remind herself to feel into the aliveness within. She then notices the sign for a tattoo parlour, 6th Sense Tattoo Studio. She's always thought she'd like to get a tattoo but never felt her body was good enough.

Oh my god, she thinks as she feels the excitement rise within. She feels drawn to go in, and at that moment, she can't think of a better way to mark that this is her body—to accept and celebrate it.

She pushes the door open. The space is neat and decorated with intricate designs along one wall. Immediately in front of her is a room divider to offer privacy. She feels nervous and excited all at once. Then she hears a female voice call out, 'Hang on a tick.'

Jenni looks at the designs blu-tacked to the wall, although she already knows what she wants.

From behind the divider, a young woman of Asian appearance appears. She has tattoos up both arms and multiple piercings in both ears. Her long hair is dyed a soft blue at the tips and is in multiple French braids loosely held together at the nape of her neck.

She smiles at Jenni. 'Howdy, I'm Nat. How can I help ya?'

'I'd like a small heart tattoo,' Jenni declares.

'You're in luck,' Nat says, 'I had a cancellation this arvo. So, if you'd like to have it done today... I can do that... Or we can discuss what you want and you come back when you're ready to do it. Up to you.'

'Oh, I'm pretty certain I know what I want.' Jenni feels even more confident she wants to do this.

'Okay, shall we have a gander at designs?' Nat asks, directing Jenni to a table behind the divider.

'Sure,' Jenni says, taking in the tattoo equipment. 'What I want is a simple heart outline. I've always liked the subtleness of it.'

'Do ya know where you'd like it?'

'On my hip or stomach... about here.' Jenni gestures to her stomach just above her knickers.

Nat pulls out three prints and places them on the table in front of Jenni. 'Yes, that's exactly what I'm looking for,' Jenni confirms, pointing to the heart in the middle.

'Well, you don't beat about the bush, do ya?' Nat grins. 'Now, you need to be one hundred per cent certain of the positioning. There's a mirror over there if you wanna try positioning the printouts and decide exactly where you want the tat and which size.' Nat hands Jenni three printouts of the heart she selected.

'Makes sense.' Jenni shoots her a smile before making her way to the mirror, separated from the rest of the room only by a low shelving unit with picture frames and magazines. She tentatively unzips her pants and pulls them down to crotch height. She takes the printout she likes and positions it where she's thinking on her stomach, just above her knicker line. She plays with positioning to determine the right size and angle.

After about five minutes, Nat pops her head around the shelving unit. 'Need any help or advice?'

Having this woman right there with her pants part of the way down would have humiliated Jenni in the past. However, right now, she could see her body as simply a canvas for her to express herself.

Nat's eyes gaze over Jenni's stomach. 'I reckon the medium heart would be flattering. Starting at your waistline.' She indicates on her own flat stomach.

Jenni can't remember when anyone had talked about anything looking *flattering* regarding her body, let alone seeing her body without a smirk of judgement. She examines her body in the mirror for its form, the curves and grooves, without an internal commentary of what should or should not be, but simply seeing it for what it is. She takes the heart and places it higher on her waist, where Nat had indicated. 'That's perfect,' Jenni exclaims, 'let's... let's do it.'

'You sure?' Nat confirms. 'It's your decision. You gotta love it and feel a connection to it.'

'Yep, I sure do,' Jenni affirms, 'I know exactly what this tattoo means to me.'

When Jenni leaves the tattoo parlour supporting an elegant heart on her stomach, she's on a *high*. She is aware of the heat from the tattoo and the pull of the wrap as she walks, but she feels so elated that she decides to wander around a little and enjoy the afternoon. She walks down the street, head high and then notices a lingerie shop: the exact kind of store that made her feel so large and so small at the same time.

Jenni feels so empowered she decides to step into the lingerie shop, merely to wander around and check out the range of their *plus-size* clothing. Nothing is likely to range to her size, but she thinks, *what the hell, I just want to see how it feels to walk into the lair of so much past pain.* She is curious to see how it will feel to enter a place where the depth of society's obsession with women looking a certain way is so apparent. A place where lingerie is presented amongst life-size photos of teens posing as women wearing sexy negligees or matching bras and panties, with expressionless faces and 'fuck me' eyes. A place where the female body is standardised, and the insidious message is that women are sexy *things*.

Jenni knows the plus-size section will provide negligible relief from the scant thongs and bras, but wants to try walking through the store without feeling shame for her body. She has barely stepped into the shop when a short blonde in a push-up bra is in front of her. *Where had she come from—was she hiding amongst the hanging bras to greet people?* Jenni muses.

'I'm sorry, but you won't find anything in your size here,' the blonde chirps.

Jenni can't believe she's come straight out and said it. She fakes a laugh. 'Oh, I'm not looking for me... I'm... I'm looking for my girlfriend,' Jenni is on a roll, 'I think she's a size six... way smaller than you.' She indicates the petite blonde's body with her eyes.

'Oh.' The blonde re-orientates herself to start again in offering her assistance. 'Is there anything in particular I can help you find?'

Does she want to get me in and out of the store as quickly as possible? Jenni wonders. *Not so fast, lady. You can't mess with this big girl.*

'Do you have anything like... edible undies?' Jenni asks, thinking on her feet.

'No.' The blonde doesn't look impressed.

Jenni decides to continue. 'Crotchless, then?' says Jenni, trying to keep a straight face.

'No,' the blonde says disbelievingly.

'Anything… for clit stimulation?' *Where had that come from?* Jenni wonders, trying her hardest not to laugh out loud.

'I'm sorry,' the blonde says hesitantly, 'I think you have the wrong type of store.'

'Really?' Jenni acts surprised. 'I thought this store was for tiny little objectified sex objects.'

The blonde stands still, a look of shock on her face, any reply frozen in her mouth.

Jenni turns, leaving the store with her head held even higher than when she'd entered. She's spent so much of her life trying to be something she didn't even want to be, all in the hope she would feel confident. She realises now she would have been swapping the stigma of being fat for conformity to the thin ideal, which would simply be another constraint. She now knows losing weight doesn't lead to confidence. But that confidence is accessible to her now, without her needing to change a thing.

As Jenni continues to the train station, she notices a book in a bookshop window—Joyful Eating. Beside it is a poster that says, "Free yourself of the struggle of eating and weight concerns with a refreshing philosophy of self-acceptance and self-care".

Curious, Jenni enters the store to take a closer look. Although the title sounds like it might just be about eating, the caption beside it indicates more. She picks up the book and flips through it, gleaming phrases like emotional eating, self-reflection, ditch food labels and diet rules, overcoming your fear of hunger and debunking your sabotaging thoughts. Although she feels empowered right now, Jenni thinks the book may reinforce some of what she's learnt. So, she decides to buy it.

That night after a shower, avoiding wetting her tattoo, Jenni prepares herself a cup of herbal tea and gets comfortable on the couch by the reading lamp. She begins reading Joyful Eating. The beginning reinforces why diets don't work. Then, when she reaches the chapter, "Are you starving yourself of happiness?" she thinks of all the things she's made conditional on her weight. She no longer wants to hold back from living her life fully because of her weight. Her body is what it is. Right now, she can move, nourish and care for the body she has.

Jenni puts the book down and pushes aside her dressing gown to reveal her tattoo still under the wrap. The tattoo is just the beginning.

Chapter 9

"When you release your fear of being judged for your weight, it can appear that those around you judge you less for it."

– Joyful Eating

Jenni doesn't tell anyone at work about the tattoo all day Tuesday, but can no longer keep it to herself by Wednesday. As her computer is loading, she wheels her chair over to Pam's desk and, in a near whisper, says, 'Guess what I did Monday night?'

'I've got no idea.' Pam raises her eyebrows, questioning Jenni.

Jenni leans in and says even quieter, 'I... I got a tattoo.' A cheeky grin spreads across her face.

'You what?' Pam shrieks in disbelief.

Still whispering, Jenni says, 'I got a tattoo. Right here.' She points to her stomach.

'I can't believe you did that,' Pam continues incredulously.

'You can't believe she did what?' Amanda asks over the divide between her and Pam's desk.

'Jenni got a tattoo!' Pam screeches, turning the heads of the staff in the glass meeting rooms.

'Shush.' Jenni motions for Pam to quieten her voice. 'I didn't want it shouted from the rooftops,' she asserts, diverting her eyes from the glass offices.

None of them notices Barry standing nearby, just to the side of Amanda's desk, searching in a filing cabinet. He's overheard Pam's exclamation and lingers, curious. He keeps his head low and pretends to keep searching.

'Why didn't you wait until you lost the weight?' Amanda asks in a judgemental tone.

'This is the body I have right now,' Jenni declares proudly.

'But it will change,' Amanda says tartly.

'Everyone's body will change,' Jenni responds, 'their skin will sag and wrinkle if they live long enough.'

Amanda frowns.

Barry smiles to himself. He picks up the file he'd come for and walks away, trying to be inconspicuous.

Only then does Jenni notice him. *Great, now Barry knows. He probably thinks it's disgusting. Fuck, I don't care what men, anyone for that matter, think of my body anymore. This is my body. I don't need to prove myself to anyone. Anyone who can't accept me as I am is not worth it,* she thinks with her eyes still set on Barry, just as Becca walks past toward the bathroom, looking distressed.

Jenni slides her chair back to her desk, signalling to the others it is time to get back to work. She has a stack of purchase orders to get through.

After about half an hour, Jenni realises Becca hasn't returned from the bathroom. She decides to check if she is okay.

Jenni hears Becca crying in one of the toilet stalls and knocks gently on the door. 'Are you okay, Bec?'

Becca opens the door. She has streaks of mascara down her cheeks. Her nose is red, and there is toilet paper strewn all over the stall.

'Oh, Becca, what's happened?' Jenni kneels, strategically placing a knee on a clean piece of toilet paper.

'He... he slept with a co-worker at a conference,' Becca sobs.

'Who, Adam?'

'Yes, the arsehole, Adam. He slept with her at a conference late last month.'

Jenni is silent, dumbfounded.

Becca explains, struggling to get the words out, 'He's heading to an interstate training next week. And I... I noticed a message come up on his phone, and I couldn't help but look. It... it was her. Her, suggesting another hot steamy night together.'

Jenni places a comforting hand on Becca's knee.

'I confronted him about it and he... he didn't deny it. He said it was a moment of weakness, that they'd been drinking in the hotel lobby and on an impulse, he invited her to his room.'

'Oh, Becca. I'm so sorry.' Jenni can't believe what she is hearing. Becca always had it so together.

'That's not the worst part!' Becca sobs with a sharpness to her voice.

Jenni nods for Becca to continue.

Becca presses her hands over her face and drags her fingertips over her eyes, smearing her mascara even more. 'I... I can't believe who it is.' She shakes her head. 'She's... she's the stocky blonde project manager.' She gestures her hands around her head in a questioning manner. 'She's got to be at least ten years older than him. I can't... I can't believe he would cheat on me with *her*.'

Despite the snarkiness in her voice, Becca is clearly frustrated and confused. 'I work so hard to be the perfect wife and mother.' She buries her face in her hands again. 'I work so hard to... to

maintain a perfect body, and he goes and sleeps with a fa...'
Becca is convulsing in tears, but realising how this must come
across to Jenni, manages to spit out an 'I'm sorry.'

Becca keeps her head down while Jenni stares directly at her,
neither of them saying a word. Eye contact or words would be
too confronting for them both, given Becca couldn't see how
Adam could be attracted to a larger, older woman; a woman not
too dissimilar to the one before her.

Becca has spent her entire life trying to be perfect, and it still
isn't good enough. Perfection is not a sure-fire way to happiness.
Jenni has come to understand that now. But kneeling here looking
at this quivering petite woman in front of her, she sees herself. Jenni
can see how Becca too, has put her happiness in others' hands and
thought it was something she could achieve by controlling her
body—she also believed she needed to look a certain way to be
happy. Jenni now knows this is not the case. It has never been.

'Come on, Becca. I think you need to get out of here. Do you
want me to tell Priya you had to go home sick?'

Becca nods without looking Jenni in the eyes.

Despite the events of the morning, Jenni is able to focus on her
work with a thoroughness she hasn't felt for a long time. Only
when she notices her stomach growling does she step away from
her desk at two o'clock.

As Jenni makes her way out of the office to pick something
up for lunch, she walks past the lunchroom and notices Norelle
sitting there, nestling a cup of tea between her hands. 'Hi,
Norelle.' Jenni waves.

'Afternoon, Jenni.' Norelle smiles.

Jenni steps into the lunchroom. 'Norelle?' Jenni gives a cheeky
smile. 'Did you hear that I got a tattoo?'

'No, I didn't!' *Never one to gossip,* Jenni thinks, smiling to herself.

'It felt like a great way to express acceptance of myself as I am right now,' Jenni declares triumphantly.

'I'm delighted that you're feeling more comfortable in your own skin, Jenni.'

'I sure am.' Jenni lingers a moment. 'I wanted to thank you for helping me see how I was starving myself of happiness and preventing myself from caring for my body the way it is. I was always fighting against it. I now know happiness is not something I can acquire through achieving an external goal. Happiness is the result of how I see the world.'

Norelle gives her a knowing smile. 'Life is only ever now, in the present moment.'

'Aha,' says Jenni as she motions towards the door, 'I've really got to get something to eat. However, I wanted to ask, I found this book called Joyful Eating by a lady named Tansy Boggon. She wouldn't happen to be the same Tansy we met at the library, would she?'

Norelle's face gives nothing away.

'That would be an incredible coincidence, wouldn't it?' Jenni states.

'It would indeed.' Norelle smiles. 'Some coincidence.'

Jenni doesn't have time to linger any longer, as she is getting quite hungry. So, she heads to a hole-in-the-wall sushi bar down the street from the Union building and orders a bento box.

In the past, she would have purchased a few pieces of sushi to take away, preferring to eat it at her desk. But today, she feels like a break from the office. She no longer feels the same shame of being seen eating—as everyone, even big girls, have to eat. She sits at a small table on the street and relishes every mouthful while watching people mill about the city.

While she's eating, Jenni's phone pings, but she ignores it until she finishes eating. When she checks the message, she is astounded to see it's a text from Becca: *I'm so sorry about this morning. I didn't mean to imply that you are undesirable. You're an incredible person, Jen.*

Jenni responds: *i understand Becca. you were upset. i didn't take it personally :-)*

Almost instantaneously, Becca replies: *thnx for your understanding. r u able to make it to the beach party nxt weekend? I'm still having it, despite this. I couldn't cancel now!*

Jenni takes a moment. She remembers how adamant she'd been with Paul that she wouldn't hang out by the pool with his colleagues' partners. But she no longer feels defined by her body, and she loves to swim. The reply she types even surprises herself: *sure, i'd love to.*

On the way home, Jenni realises she'll have to purchase a new swimsuit to replace the old saggy black coverup she's owned for as long as she can remember. She decides rather than scouring plus-size stores in the city, she'll buy something online. If she orders it tonight, she'll have it in time for Becca's beach party.

She searches specialty websites with plus size swimwear and stumbles across sites where plus-size women share images of their bodies in a variety of swimwear, declaring they don't need to lose weight to be beach-ready.

Jenni has heard of the body-positive movement but, until now, has ignored it as she hadn't acknowledged it is okay to celebrate the body you have. She finds herself scrolling through Facebook pages and blogs of women unapologetically displaying their bodies in swimsuits and stylish get-ups. Before she knows it, an hour has passed. It is inspirational, but she has to remind herself of the task at hand—purchasing a swimsuit.

She decides on a site and searches the selection of colourful one-pieces, swim dresses, tankinis and bikinis. She selects a two-piece high-waisted swimsuit in a floral design with a frilled top. It provides support but has a flattering low scoop neckline.

Jenni then rummages through the hallway drawer to find her tape measure to compare her measurements to the sizing chart. She wraps the tape measure around her hips and records the measurement on a post-it note. She then proceeds to do the same for her waist and bust. However, unlike all the previous times she's wrapped this tape measure around her body to take 'before' and 'after' measurements, she is now taking an impartial measure of her size. It feels so matter-of-fact rather than hopeful or shameful—it simply is what it is.

Jenni adds an open front coral-coloured kaftan to the order and puts through the purchase. She then heads to bed, looking forward to the feeling of swimming in the open ocean.

⌒⌒

'G-o-o-d M-o-r-n-i-n-g,' Jenni sings to Pam as she sits down at her desk.

'Why, hello. You're particularly cheery today,' Pam states.

'I've really come to realise we believe we are the only ones with struggles, fears and doubt. We all do. Time to let it go,' Jenni says philosophically.

'Well, that's deep for a Thursday,' Pam observes, 'you've become quite the philosopher lately.'

'I'm just seeing life differently, that's all,' Jenni muses.

'What I'm seeing looks a little different, too.' Pam indicates the floral silk scarf loosely draped around Jenni's neck.

'Yes. I'm going to brighten up my wardrobe a little. Last night, I even purchased a floral swimsuit for Becca's party.'

Pam looks confused. 'Oh, are you going?'

'Yes,' Jenni says confidently, 'I love swimming. I just haven't been for ages and I needed to replace my old daggy one piece. You coming?' she asks Pam.

'Oh, I don't know if I'd go. It's not the sort of thing Brian would want to go to.'

'Well, you can come on your own. I'm not going with anyone.'

'I don't know… Brian prefers quiet weekends.'

'But you don't always have to do what Brian wants,' Jenni suggests with a smirk, 'what… what would you like to do?'

Pam looks uncertain. Jenni realises that just like she has used her weight, Pam uses Brian as an excuse to hold herself back. She reflects on how it is sometimes easier to use something as an excuse not to face our fears and admit what we truly want. *Why do we do this to ourselves?* Jenni wonders.

'I'm hardly beach body ready,' Pam admits.

'You got bathers?' Jenni asks.

Pam nods.

'A hat? Sunglasses? Sandals?' Jenni continues, 'well, you're beach body ready, then.' Jenni grins.

Pam pokes her tongue out at Jenni. 'Okay, okay. I get it.' A smile starts to appear on her face. 'I'll go.'

Jenni claps her hands together like an excited child. 'Yay!'

'Let's go together. I'll drive you,' Pam offers.

'Well, that's perfect.' Jenni smirks. 'Given that, I don't have a car.'

⁓

At midday, Jenni is sitting in the lunchroom on her own when Barry enters. She glances up to see who it is and then draws her attention back to her lunch. Barry heads for the fridge and pauses a moment. 'Jenni?'

'Mm-hmm,' she acknowledges him with her mouth full of salad.

'I just wanted to say... I thought it was... terrific... the way you stood up for yourself against Amanda yesterday.'

'Oh. Thanks, Barry.' Jenni is not sure what else to say. He hadn't thought what she'd assumed. Yet, she is still unsure what business it is of his.

'Can I join you?' He indicates the chair opposite Jenni.

'Sure, help yourself.' She shrugs.

Barry sits across the table from Jenni and opens his lunchbox. He gives an uneasy smile when she looks up from her salad. *For a man who deals with clients all day, he sure looks awkward,* she thinks.

'It looks like we both managed to pack a lunch today.' Jenni observes, breaking the heavy silence.

'Yep. Leftovers.' Barry indicates his lunchbox. 'Are you going to Becca's beach party next weekend?' he asks.

'I wasn't, but just yesterday, I decided I would.'

'Oh, I'm pleased you're going—it will give me someone rational to hang out with,' he says.

'You think I'm rational?'

'Well, more rational than some other people.' He smiles wider than before. Jenni notices a dimple on his left cheek. Barry has always been friendly toward Jenni, but she senses something else. She shifts in her seat. Barry continues, 'You know what I mean... it's going to be a huge song and dance for a child's fifth birthday. Even the fact that we're invited—colleagues. It seems to be a lot of hoopla for a kid's party.'

'Hoopla?' Jenni raises an eyebrow at Barry and laughs.

'You know what I mean!'

'I know.' She smiles. 'I don't disagree with you. It will probably be a bohemian mermaid or underwater princess theme.'

'Thankfully, we haven't been asked to dress up. I'm not sure I have what it takes to be a merman. That's right, isn't it—a merman?'

'Oh, yes, I can see you as a merman. Barry—creature of the sea.'

'Let's not put that image into our minds.' He laughs.

'Yes, let's not,' Jenni corroborates. 'I haven't been to the beach for such a long time, so this party is a great excuse to go.'

'And a great excuse to show off that new tattoo of yours.' Barry grins at her.

'Oh, I'll probably have to keep it covered. It's still healing—not really supposed to swim with it... Anyway, I didn't get the tattoo to show it off to anyone—it's for me.'

'I know. I think it's great. People worry too much about what other people think of them and never learn to be just themselves. And yet... it is someone's uniqueness, their quirkiness, which makes them so... interesting.' Barry concentrates on his lunch and takes a mouthful so he has an excuse not to say anything further that will dig him into a hole.

Jenni agrees, 'I think you're right, Barry. We can spend so much of our lives trying to be who we think everyone else wants us to be and yet lose ourselves. You know... I think it is part of the issue with this beach party Becca is organising. I wonder if she is trying to do everything *right*. Yet nothing can ever be good enough. I suppose, in the end, that's why I decided to go—to support her. And because I think we all have the same insecurities that we aren't good enough or have to be a better version of ourselves to be acceptable or likeable.'

'When you are likeable, just as you are,' he announces.

Did he just say that? Jenni smiles at him. In the past, she would have brushed off compliments like that, thinking she didn't deserve it, but right now, she accepts it. 'Thank you, Barry.'

Barry and Jenni gaze at each other when in walk Rachel and Mora, who both work in customer service alongside Becca. They both have children and are clearly talking about the beach party also. They smile at Barry and Jenni and sit down at another table in the lunchroom.

'Do you want to share a ride to the party?' Barry asks Jenni, which catches the attention of Rachel and Mora.

Mora calls over, 'Are you both coming next weekend?'

'We sure are,' Barry responds, 'I'm pretty sure the entire office was invited.'

Mora's face clearly shows disbelief. *What because the office nerd and fatty are coming to the party also?* Jenni thinks. Living in a larger body, she realises that other people's judgement will always be something she'll have to face. However, it occurs to her that what other people think of her has nothing to do with her.

'We're really looking forward to it. It should be a lot of fun. Who doesn't love a kid's beach party?' Jenni calls across the room. She then turns back to Barry. 'I'm good for a ride.'

'Oh, okay... thought I'd offer.' He is clearly pondering what to say next. Then he leans towards Jenni and says quietly so the others can't hear, 'I look forward to hanging out—having someone I can have a decent conversation and laugh with.' He nods toward Mora and Rachel.

'It sure will be a laugh—to see how extravagant an affair it is,' Jenni says quietly. Only then realising she'd used the word *affair*.

'It sure will.' Barry beams, sitting back and looking at Jenni.

It has been such a long time since someone has shown interest in her that she isn't sure what this is. *Is Barry merely being friendly or is there more to this?* she wonders. It occurs to Jenni that just as she has shrugged off compliments, she rarely interprets anyone's behaviour as possible interest in her.

She shoots him a smile before placing the lid on her salad container. 'I'd better get back to work. I look forward to your company at the party.'

'Me too.' Barry grins.

Jenni feels a little self-conscious as she leaves the lunchroom. However, it is not the feeling of being judged she has become accustomed to. It is a feeling of being seen.

※

Mid-afternoon, Priya makes her way briskly to Jenni's desk. 'You aren't busy on Saturday, are you?'

Why would she assume I'm not busy? thinks Jenni, although she doesn't have any plans. 'No, not really.'

'Mora can no longer support Norelle at the school fete we've sponsored this weekend. She's had a family thing come up. Could you step in?'

'Oh... okay. Sure.'

'You're a lifesaver, Jenni. Becca's busy with moving and party preparations and Rachel and Mora have activities with their kids planned. It would really help Norelle out to have an extra set of hands there just to answer questions and give out Union balloons and other merchandise. She normally does some kind of competition.'

'No worries.'

'Okay, that's sorted,' Priya says, making a move, 'just check in with Norelle as to what she requires, but I think it should be pretty straightforward.'

'Sure,' Jenni responds, as Priya is already on her way down the stairs—always in a rush somewhere.

※

Jenni wakes early on Saturday morning as she's going to help Norelle set up the stand at the fete. She searches her wardrobe for something colourful to set the tone for the day. She wants to dress in something fun as she's going to be spending the day interacting with children.

She wriggles into stretchy black pants, given that black is all she has, and then decides to put on a pink workout tee-shirt she's rarely worn and wouldn't normally wear out. It is the sort of thing she'd previously only considered wearing to workout in— if she were to workout. She then wraps a scarf with a colourful print around her wrist and puts on a cotton beaded necklace she can only guess her mother gave her or made for her. She then grabs a straw fedora hat and, popping it on her head, takes in the eclectic combination of her outfit.

Jenni spends the morning working alongside Norelle, talking with the public, giving out balloons and helping kids with a maths activity that will enter them in the draw for an education fun pack. She finds herself getting into the community spirit, laughing and joking with parents as they come past.

Then late morning, a young teacher with long straight brown hair comes over to their stall. 'I was wondering,' she begins, 'whether one of you could join our teacher's three-legged race? We thought it would be fun to have an adults' race after the kids go, but it seems the book auction is going overtime.'

'Oh, okay.' Jenni looks to Norelle.

'How about you go,' Norelle says to Jenni, 'I'll be fine on my own.'

'You sure?' Jenni says, feeling in the community spirit.

'If you wanted,' the brunette teacher says, 'you could both go. I'm happy to hold the fort here for a bit if you'd like to go together.'

Jenni and Norelle exchange a glance, a smile spreading across their faces. 'We'd love to if you're sure you don't mind,' Norelle says.

'Absolutely not,' the teacher replies convincingly.

'Okay, let's do this,' says Norelle, clapping her hands together.

'Let's,' says Jenni as she takes a sip from her water bottle and then follows Norelle to where the three-legged race is.

An official male teacher explains the rules and hands them a short physio stretch band to tie their legs together. They then head to the start line.

Norelle bends down to tie their legs together with the physio stretch band. Then when she stands, Jenni wraps her arm around Norelle's tiny waist, and Norelle takes hold of Jenni's shoulder. They limp around a bit to get in sync with one another, laughing as Jenni pulls Norelle's leg forward, causing her to hop her back foot along to balance herself. After a few feeble attempts, they hobble over to the start line, where the others are also readying themselves for the race.

'Okay, teams, are we all good to go?' one of the teachers asks. They glance at one another and then turn to the start line with determination on their faces.

The adjudicator gives a confirmation nod and then calls, 'On your mark, get set, go!'

Norelle and Jenni lurch forward over the start line alongside four other pairs, all hobbling and laughing as they pull at one another. One team pulls apart from one another and falls to the ground in laughter and another—clearly an athletic pair—bound forward in perfect synchronicity.

Jenni and Norelle step, hobble and hop slowly and steadily, balancing one another as they make their way to the finish line. Jenni giggles loudly whenever they move out of sync and have to regroup to move their legs in time. They are so focused on each step that the usual thought of those watching or being the only big girl in the race doesn't enter Jenni's mind.

Then, as they take their final step over the finish line in second place, they look up to see Barry cheering loudly. 'Well done, ladies!' He claps.

'Thanks, Barry!' they say in unison, grinning like children. Norelle and Jenni hug each other and shimmy their feet out of the band.

Looking at Barry, Jenni says, 'I didn't know you were coming.'

'Oh, I wasn't going to and then I thought it's such a nice day. Why not come out and see what you and Norelle are up to?' He grins.

'And you happened to find us when we were away from our stall!' Norelle exclaims.

'Oh, you weren't hard to find. I could hear your infectious laughter a mile off,' he says, looking to Jenni.

Jenni plays wounded. 'That bad, huh?'

'Not my words.' Barry smirks.

'Well, I'd better get back to our stand,' Norelle says, also beginning to feel something else is going on here. She turns to Jenni. 'Take your time getting back to the stand. I can manage on my own for a bit.'

'You sure?' Jenni asks.

'Absolutely. Enjoy some of the fete together, you two.' She pats Jenni on the shoulder. 'Thanks for the race.'

'You too,' Jenni says, avoiding eye contact with Barry, not knowing what to do now.

Barry breaks the silence. 'I saw one of those strawberries and cream vans on my way over here.'

'Oh, yes, those strawberries look super fresh,' Jenni comments.

'Can I shout you a serve of strawberries and cream?' Barry tilts his head towards her.

'Absolutely!' Jenni confirms, completely forgetting the discomfort of eating in front of anyone else that she's felt for most of her life.

Barry and Jenni walk towards the van, and he orders two small serves of strawberries and cream. 'Chocolate sauce?' he asks.

'Umm, no. Just cream. Thanks.'

He passes her the tub, and she scoops up a strawberry and dollop of cream and places it in her mouth. 'Oh, that is SOOO good!' she exclaims with her mouth still full.

'Delicious, huh?' he says, grinning as he takes a mouthful. 'Mm... mm... mm,' he says. 'Shall we?' He nods towards the other stalls.

They begin walking together, their tubs of strawberries and cream in hand, looking at the stalls and games.

'Okay, so I now know you like strawberries and cream,' Barry says, 'what are some other duos you think work?' he asks.

Jenni licks her lips for any traces of cream. 'You mean like peanut butter and jam?'

'I suppose it could be food or non-food duos,' he confirms.

'Food... I'd have to say coffee and toffee,' Jenni says with little hesitation.

'Oh, okay.' Barry considers it a moment. 'I can get on board with that.'

'What's a food duo you like?' she asks.

'Um... avocado toast has got to be up there.' He continues to think.

'Not vegemite?' Jenni questions.

'Well, I wouldn't say no. But it's not my go-to of toast condiments.'

'No? So, you're not a true blue Aussie bloke then?'

'Not exactly,' he admits, 'I'm a true blue Aussie, but I don't think anyone would mistake me for a blokey bloke.'

'Oh, really?' Jenni gives him a quizzical look. 'I had you pegged as a beer and footie kind of guy.' She shoots him a cheeky smile.

'If that's what you expected, you'll be very disappointed here,' he says.

'Yes, very disappointing,' she says, giving him a shy smile. Then noticing the cone toss, she continues, 'Come on Barry, show me your manliness.'

'I think that's for kids,' he says.

'Oh, you too much of a man for a kid's game?' she teases.

'Never said I was mature,' Barry says, taking hold of three colourful rings. 'Shall we?' he challenges her.

'You betcha,' she says, picking up three rings herself.

'Are we betting?' he asks.

'Umm, it was just a phrase… but we could bet. Winner, mmm… I'm not sure,' Jenni looks to him for ideas.

'Loser sits with Amanda at Becca's party.' Barry ventures.

Jenni nudges him. 'You are so bad.'

'Never said I was good.'

'But you're the good boy in the office,' she teases.

'That's only in the office, though. You haven't got to know me outside of work,' he dares.

'Nor you, me,' Jenni says, handing him her remaining strawberries.

She throws one ring that tumbles to the ground in front of the cone. Her second attempt isn't much better. However, she gets her final ring onto the cone. Barry laughs, and she grabs her strawberries from him in a playful pout.

'Step aside,' Barry says, 'allow me to show you how it's done.'

'Okay,' Jenni tuts.

Barry stands on the distance line with a serious look on his face. He eyes the cone and aligns his body and arm. Jenni remains quiet as he skilfully flicks each ring onto the cone.

'Wow, that was impressive. You're quite competitive, aren't you?' she observes.

'Sure am.' He grins. 'Although it's a shame you'll be sitting with Amanda next weekend.' He brings his index finger to his cheek as if thinking. 'I'll just have to sit opposite you then, won't I?'

'You will,' Jenni says, turning to make her way over to the stand Norelle is manning.

Chapter 10

"... you are worthy of self-acceptance and self-care as you are, right now, since your weight does not reflect your self-worth."

— Joyful Eating

෨෨

The following week Jenni waits patiently for the swimwear to arrive. When it does, she rips it open like a child at Christmas. She hasn't bought something beautiful for herself—for the body she has now—well, ever.

She takes out the soft coral-coloured kaftan and holds it up to her face. It compliments her complexion.

Now for the moment of truth: the swimsuit.

She pulls out the bottoms, admiring the beautiful colours and then places them against herself, spreading them hip to hip. They look like they should fit. She takes out the top and then removes her clothing.

She stands naked in front of the mirror. Yet she is no longer judging what she sees—this is her, the body she inhabits to live her life full out.

She then pulls on the bottoms. It is a snug fit, but they don't dig in too much and come up high to her belly button. She turns to check out her butt cheeks—mostly covered.

She then brings the bikini top over her head, shuffles her breasts into place and does up the clasp at the side. It gives her flattering cleavage, and she plays with the straps that can be on or off the shoulder.

She stands side on and looks at herself in this bright, colourful bikini. She hasn't seen herself in anything like this since she was a child; it is feminine and playful. Her stomach sticks out a little between the bottom and top, but that is just the way her body is; everything is appropriately covered and in place.

Jenni then takes the kaftan and slides it over her shoulders, doing up the small tie at the front. It is actually somewhat seductive, giving a silhouette of the bikini beneath and showing her cleavage and a strip of leg. She swirls around in it like a child about to go to a bohemian mermaid birthday party. She is beach ready!

Saturday afternoon, Pam arrives at Jenni's apartment to head to Becca's party. Jenni is ready to go. She's already got her bathers and kaftan on, sun hat and sunscreen ready, along with a change of clothes if she decides to take a dip.

'Wow, look at you, Miss Resort Holiday! Don't you look the part?' Pam shrieks when Jenni opens her front door.

'Oh, yes, I sure am ready for the beach,' Jenni states confidently. She can't remember the last time she was excited to don bathers and spend time at the beach.

'Well, I needn't ask if you're ready. You couldn't look more ready.' Pam smiles, trying to comprehend the vision before her—a radiant and excited Jenni.

'Yep,' Jenni chirps. 'Let me grab the flowers, and I can come right down.'

Jenni emerges from her apartment with a large, crocheted raffia beach bag slung over her shoulder and an arrangement of flowers in shades of white, peach and silvery green, beautifully arranged in a weathered wooden planter box.

Pam's jaw drops. 'Oh, Jenni, they're gorgeous! Very… bohemian.'

'That's what I was going for.' Jenni smiles, slightly chuffed at her creation.

'You made it?' Pam exclaims. 'It looks like something you'd get at a florist. It's beautiful, Jenni.'

'Ahh, thanks. Let's go.'

☙

As Pam negotiates her way out of the city, she comments, 'I didn't know you could arrange flowers?' She gives Jenni a quizzical sidewards glance. 'How long have we known each other?'

'I know. It's something I haven't done for a really long time. As a child, I loved all things craft,' Jenni confesses, 'I particularly loved anything to do with colour—different shades, accents, complementary colours, that sort of thing.'

'Well,' Pam pauses as she negotiates a roundabout, 'you've got real talent.'

Jenni smiles. Whether or not she has talent, she definitely wants to explore her passion. 'Yes, I think I'll pursue more creative projects.'

'You definitely should,' Pam says encouragingly.

'What about you? Do you have a hobby you enjoy or used to?' Jenni asks.

'Mm… not really, what with work, housework, Brian, there isn't a lot of spare time.'

'Do you do anything just for you?' I only ask because even though I don't have a partner or kids, I often didn't take the time to do something purely for enjoyment. You know… something that lights me up.'

'I sure have noticed a shift in you lately,' Pam comments, turning momentarily to Jenni.

Jenni smiles. 'I want to bring more colour into my life—take more time to smell the roses, as they say. Norelle has really helped me see how I was often in my own head.'

'It's really wonderful to see you happier, Jenni. Hey, look at us, heading to Becca's beach party. Who would've ever guessed?'

'I know, right?'

'I'm really pleased you talked me into this,' Pam says, 'you're right. I do need to get out of the house a bit more and do things for myself. Brian likes quiet time to himself and prefers to stay home after a tiring week at work. However, as you know, I'm more extroverted and do enjoy time socialising.'

Jenni nods and indicates for her to continue.

'I've spent years doing what he wants. When the kids were young, I didn't notice it so much as there was always something happening; someone visiting, some event to taxi the kids to, that sort of thing. I really enjoyed that time in my life. However, now they're older and don't need me or want me around so much, life has become a lot quieter.' She turns towards Jenni momentarily. 'So, thanks for getting me out of the house. I'm ready to let my hair down and have a good night.'

'Me too,' Jenni agrees.

Pam continues, 'Given that I'm designated driver, I'll leave the drinking to you, but I'm going to enjoy the delectable spread Becca's prepared. I've heard all week about what she's preparing—sounds somewhat healthy but delicious.'

'I know, it sounds like she's prepared a feast,' Jenni agrees. Then she continues, 'That's the other thing I've really learnt, is to relish every mouthful. I think before, I ate to rebel against the rules, or I'd eat because I would soon have to go without or because I was feeling sad or annoyed. Now, I've learnt to relish every mouthful.'

'But *bad* food is *so* good.' Pam smirks.

'But that's the thing I've realised; just thinking it's *bad* made me want to eat it more and eat it at times when it wasn't serving me in any way—other than to drown out my thoughts or emotions.'

'Hmmm... tell me more,' Pam says as they get onto the highway. Jenni continues happily jabbering the entire trip to the beach, recounting some of her conversations with Norelle.

When Pam and Jenni arrive at the beach party, their jaws drop; it is everything they expected and more. Tables are set up on the beach under umbrellas and teepees, where fairy lights hang. On the sand are colourful rugs and throw cushions. It is over the top but also quite spectacular, just like everything that Becca does—nothing in half measures.

In the past, Jenni wouldn't have been caught dead at such an event. But now, she doesn't care. She loves to swim. And she plans to focus on being in good company, the delicious food and the sensations of being right there by the ocean, sand beneath her feet and the sea breeze on her skin. She is just going to be herself. Who else could she be, anyway? Who had she been trying to fool all these years?

'Shall we?' Pam gestures to the teepees.

'Let's,' Jenni says, walking towards the tables, holding her flower arrangement.

'Well, hello ladies,' they hear Barry behind them, slightly out of breath. 'I saw you pull up and thought I'd try to catch up.' He looks to Jenni. 'I didn't realise it was Pam you were coming with. How... how are you both?'

'Great.' Jenni smiles.

'Well, this is something,' he says, gesturing to the party before them.

'It sure is,' Pam says as they continue to walk towards the setup.

As they approach the tables, Becca raises her arms and whoops as she sees the three of them. 'I'm so happy that you're here,' she says, giving them a hug in turn.

Jenni hands Becca the wooden box of flowers and Becca shrieks again. 'Oh, Jenni, they're beautiful. Where did you get them?'

'I arranged them,' Jenni humbly states as Barry and Becca's jaws drop.

Pam nods knowingly. 'Incredible, hey? The girl's got talent.'

Barry smiles. 'She sure does.'

'Oh, Jenni, they're gorgeous. Thank you.' Becca reaches forward and kisses Jenni on the cheek and then whispers, 'Thanks for everything.' She gently squeezes Jenni's arm before explaining to them the setup of the party.

She then pours them each an interesting looking aqua-coloured drink. 'I thought I'd start the evening off with something healthier,' she says, oblivious to the uncertain eyes watching her. 'It's celery and pineapple juice with blue spirulina and coconut cream. It's something of a pina colada mocktail.' Possibly, because of their unsure looks, Becca clarifies, 'We're just starting with something cleansing and hydrating. We'll get to the *real stuff* later,' she assures them with a smile.

Barry gives a gesture to gag and bends towards Jenni's ear. 'I really hope that there is some real stuff because I'm not sure I could go the entire evening on mermaid juice.'

Jenni elbows him in the ribs. 'Behave you!'

'What can I say? I came for a party,' he says cheekily.

Jenni glances at him and states with conviction, 'Oh, it's a party—just Becca style.'

And there is plenty of real stuff to come—eskies of beers, sparkling wine and soft drinks, platters of BBQ meats and vegetables arranged amongst colourful salads.

There are a lot of people at the party Jenni doesn't know. So, she continues standing with Pam and Barry, sipping the mocktail, which tastes surprisingly better than it sounded. She then notices Norelle arrive and excuses herself.

With her crocheted raffia beach bag still on her shoulder, Jenni walks towards Norelle. When they reach one another, Jenni drops her bag to the ground and hugs Norelle. As she pulls away, Jenni looks her directly in the eyes. 'Norelle, before we get into party mode, I wanted to thank you for how much you've helped me these past weeks. I don't know where I'd be without you—definitely not at a beach party wearing a bikini!' she laughs. She then reaches into her bag and hands Norelle a small black cardboard box.

'Oh, my! What is this, Jenni?' Norelle glances at her quizzically.

Jenni just looks at her expectantly, waiting for Norelle to open the box. Norelle's jaw drops when she sees inside a delicate paper filigree rose brooch made with a page from a book.

'Wow, Jenni! It's gorgeous!' Norelle exclaims.

'I made it to represent the love and learning I have received from you. Thank you, Norelle,' Jenni sincerely says as she pulls her into another embrace. 'I found my flow.'

When it's time to enjoy dinner, the guests serve themselves at the side buffet-style table and then take their seats. Jenni sits down beside Pam with her plate piled high. She then turns as Mora sits to her other side, announcing her arrival with a flurry. 'What a lovely party. I'm so hungry. Those kids have had me chasing them around all afternoon. I came up early—

designated supervisor at the pool. Have you looked around the house yet?'

'Oh, no, we haven't,' Jenni responds. 'We came straight over to the beach when we parked.'

'Oh, you'll have to take a look after dinner,' Mora gushes, 'it is spectacular! It has a spacious white kitchen and floor to ceiling windows all round. It is incredible! They're going to love having their weekends here.'

Is she unaware of Adam's infidelity? Jenni thinks. Then wonders, *maybe Becca and Adam have worked through it?* It isn't really her business, but Mora seems oblivious.

Barry then, plate in hand, makes to sit opposite Jenni. 'I believe this is my seat,' he says, 'I'm not sure the seating arrangement is exactly as agreed. But it works.' He shoots Jenni a cheeky grin.

'Do you get the feeling there is an inside joke between these two?' Mora says, leaning past Jenni to Pam.

'Something's going on between those two,' Pam says.

Jenni smiles and directs her eyes towards her lap. She momentarily wonders, *is there? Could there be?* She pushes the thought aside and composes herself. Glancing up, she turns to Mora. 'So, which of the kiddos are yours?'

Jenni allows herself to enjoy the evening with minimal internal dialogue. She savours everyone's company, and the spread of delectable food Becca has so carefully selected, prepared and displayed. Jenni places her attention on the hum of conversation, laughter and lapping of waves at the shore, not far from where they sit. She feels the breeze on her warm, sticky skin.

As darkness surrounds them, Jenni feels drawn to the water's edge. She excuses herself from the table and walks toward the ocean. She feels the breeze sweeping through her hair and the soft sand under her feet and between her toes. She drops her coral-coloured kaftan to the sand and inches her way into the water. She feels it rise up her legs, groin and stomach until she lets herself relax and be held by the water. She feels a weightlessness, not only in her body but of her soul.

Jenni floats, reflecting on how much she has postponed until she had the body she desired, until she felt her body was *good enough. Good enough for what?* she thinks. *Fuck that! I'm going to live my fucking life,* she declares to herself.

Swimming over the gentle waves, Jenni feels immense joy and aliveness within her. It occurs to her this is her life's purpose... to feel alive in each moment.

She floats there for some time, feeling the ocean water surrounding her body. Then, with a sense of internal resolve, she slowly swims back to shore. She sees the party's lights shimmering on the ocean's surface and up the sand to where the waves lap at the shore. There appears to be a figure further up the beach, but Jenni can't make out who.

She doesn't try to determine who it is. She doesn't care anymore who sees her body. Swimming is no longer about how her body looks and what others think of her. Swimming is about the sense of lightness and freedom she feels.

Jenni skims her feet on the sand below and wriggles her toes into it. Then she arches her head back to feel her hair float around her face one last time. She lifts her head so that her hair is flat away from her face. She then straightens her legs, feeling her feet sink into the soft sand. With each step up the beach in the swash, she feels the sink and plug of her feet in the sand. Then the prickle of the breeze against her damp, salty skin. She turns to face the breeze a moment, feeling it surround her entire body.

She feels a slight shiver as she heads for her kaftan. Only as she gets closer to it does she realise the silhouette is standing by her kaftan. It is Barry.

She smiles at him as she approaches.

'Jenni,' he says, gently smiling at her. 'You... you looked so peaceful out there,' he continues, stretching out his arm, holding her towel.

Jenni steps closer. Yet he doesn't hand her the towel.

Barry wraps the towel around her shoulders. His hands linger there a moment. 'What... what were you thinking about while you were swimming?'

'Not much. I just felt so free in the water.' Jenni feels her shoulders relax as she wipes them dry. 'I wasn't thinking much at all. It was more like I was washing away many of the worries that no longer serve me.'

She gives him a knowing smile as she wraps the towel around herself tightly to absorb the moisture from her bikini. She feels the prickle of drying saltwater on her legs and shoulders. Then she continues, 'Mostly... I was focused on the feeling of the water caressing my skin.' Jenni looks away a moment, a little embarrassed by her sensual description of swimming. She picks up her kaftan and wriggles into it, holding the towel with one hand.

When she turns toward Barry, she notices the dimple forming on his cheek. 'Jenni, you are a mysterious woman,' he says, breaking into a full smile. 'That... unconditional love you spoke of a few weeks back... it wasn't for someone else, was it?' he asks hopefully.

'No,' Jenni grins, leaning towards him. 'It was only ever for me.'

'It was only ever you,' he says as he pulls her into a tight embrace.

They then turn and head back to the party. Barry places his hand on the small of her back. Jenni feels the warmth of his hand and herself relax.

Acknowledgments

I began writing The Weight of a Woman while working on the final edits of my self-help book, Joyful Eating: How to Break Free of Diets and Make Peace with Your Body. I had no idea what I was doing, having never written fiction before.

At first, I simply wrote for myself because it was a story I was moved to write. I had no idea whether it would be publishable.

It was when, a good year later, I found a publisher for my children's book that I decided to revisit the novel. I wasn't sure if they would want to publish it, but I thought the only way to find out was to complete and share it.

After a few months of rewriting and edits, I emailed the manuscript to my publisher for feedback. And to my delighted surprise, the response I got was, 'we want to publish it'. I am grateful for their belief in me and bringing the book out into the world.

My deepest thanks go to the person who has always believed in me—my husband, Rob. You encouraged me to keep writing and have supported my dream to become a novelist and children's book author. It is your observation of how writing lights me up and your constant cheering me on to keep writing that has brought me to this point where I now have a beautiful book to share with readers. You have helped me shake my self-doubt and, hopefully, the self-doubt of all those who enjoy this book. I love you.

And to you, reading these words, I thank you. Although I wrote this book because it was a joy to do so, it was knowing that you may gain some insight and joy from this book that inspired me to take it all the way to publication and now into your hands. Thank you!

About the Author

Find out more about Tansy's books and sign up for her e-newsletter at:
www.joyfuleatingnutrition.com

Follow Tansy:
Instagram @tansy_joyfuleating
Facebook @joyfuleatingwithtansy

Tansy Boggon is a non-fiction, fiction and children's book author, sharing stories and philosophies to help people break free of diet rules and false beliefs to enjoy food and be themselves without guilt and shame.

She is a university-qualified nutritionist, food writer and recipe developer who incorporates mindful eating, eating psychology and a non-diet approach into her writing.

Tansy is an Australian who now calls Christchurch, New Zealand home, and enjoys yoga, dancing, experimenting in the kitchen and outdoor adventures on foot and bike.

Please write a review
Did you enjoy this story? Help others find The Weight of a Woman by leaving a short review on your preferred online store.

Thank you!

Shawline Publishing Group Pty Ltd

www.shawlinepublishing.com.au

SHAWLINE
PUBLISHING
GROUP